StarDr

Spiderboy

StarDrome 2024

SpiderBoy

BY
Rosie Trakostanec

White Elk Medicine Woman

www.bookstandpublishing.com

Published by
Bookstand Publishing
Morgan Hill, CA 95037
3915_2

Copyright © 2013 by Rosie Trakostanec
All rights reserved. No part of this publication may be reproduced or transmitted in any form or by any means, electronic or mechanical, including photocopy, recording, or any information storage and retrieval system, without permission in writing from the copyright owner.

ISBN 978-1-61863-540-2
Library of Congress Control Number: 2013939466

Printed in the United States of America

Introduction

The Old World is inhabitable; the journey begins now for the children. They were prepared for centuries through the masters and elders, to get ready for this day. It's time to let the parents and guardians know we must leave. The old world is dying and she has run out of water and the vegetation is gone. The greed has become insane amongst the people.

Many people perished and few remain, the parents and the ones before them have chosen this birth right. As the old one, I choose to stay and help the ones who remain. Then I must leave in the last pod, designed by me and other masters.

The young children have been taught since birth, the time is here.

To leave with a parent or guardian, we as humankind have been prepared for a long time by the stars. I have trained many old souls, to be ready for this day.

I come to realize that I'm not alone in this great change; my parents and grandparents have taught me well as I grew.

Spirit has shown me many things through my visions and through the fire. The ancestors have spoken of a time to come and it is now;

I'm Master Silver Cloud and this is my new beginning, to finish what was destined.

By creating a new earth, where we share the many 'gifts' of our ancestors; through our future generations. By working with our telepathic, telekinesis' energies we will live strong. This is where I and other masters will see our shape-shifters come to life and grow with love.

Only high vibrational energy flows in the new world, through our teachings and the co –creative energies of all cell souls. According to the laws of the universe; the journey begins to the new world.

ACKNOWLEDGEMENTS

Dedicated to my children and grand children

I thank creator, the grandmothers and grandfathers, angels, ark angels; high ascended ones and all my helpers from the Other Side. I thank all the souls who feel inspired by me. I thank my family, friends and the community. It takes practice to walk in spirit and continue my journey writing. I thank myself for being persistent, patient and for listening.

I admire all writers, beginners who trust in their work and all authors before me. I always felt driven to write a series of novels and envision them becoming a movie etc.; I love the energy and enthusiasm that comes with creating characters and a story. It's like raising babies that is why I dedicate this novel and the ones that follow, to my children, grandchildren and all children.

This way as souls, we can honor who we are through our unique abilities. We are all born with 'spiritual gifts' to see hear and sense our surroundings and the people in it. To grow up and be taught by an elder or mentor is important to our success; especially if we were born as old souls.

Therefore, through this novel you'll read and learn to grasp the very thing many are afraid of 'Our individual power', so we can stand in what we know as 'true self' spirit. We as souls were born with gifts' of sight, sound and hearing, so we can mature those gifts and honor them. Either through crystals, energy healing or chants etc.

With love and light to all future generations, honor who you are, as you choose your path wisely; always choose to follow your intuition.

I also love and thank my friend Sandra H/Grandmother Yellow Moon and her husband Michael for their love and support with this novel and all things 'spirit'.

With blessings,
White Elk Medicine Woman
May Spirit guide you always!

Table of Contents

Introduction   v

Acknowledgements   vii

Chapter - 1- The Pod   1

Chapter - 2– Sly Awakens   21

Chapter 3 – Sly Mentors   35

Chapter -4 – Master Silver Cloud   49

Chapter - 5 – Crystal Girl and Panther Struts   76

Chapter - 6– Shape Shifters Gather   94

Chapter - 7– StarDrome's Secret   120

Chapter - 8– The North Side – Block D   138

Chapter - 9– Disappearances   167

Chapter - 10 – Book of Truth   175

Chapter - 11 – Angel and Louise   179

Chapter – 12 – The Energy of StarDrome   185

Chapter – 13 - The Core   189

Chapter – 14 – Celebrations   195

Chapter – 15 – Luna and SpiderBoy   201

Chapter – 16 -   The Bad Lands   209

My Blessings   211

About the Author   214

1

The Pod

The Arrival

The year is 2024 and the cell souls have left the old world and are travelling in pods. As cell souls we are finally landing on this new planet in all directions: There are many different colored shaped pods; each pod holds a family of survivors. That was left over when old earth was dissolved, many must inhabit new planets, new places, and start again.

This time with new skin, telekinesis energies and telepathic sound waves, the souls will learn to adapt to a new reality. All the cell souls are slowly starting to awaken; it's strange because they can't use their mouths. They could hear themselves talking, but their jaws weren't moving and their words were heard quickly and telepathically.

But it is only through telepathic frequencies the cells speak to each other. They must relearn and be taught to stay clear and focused. So they can teach the future generations, their children, how to survive. By adapting to a new race, a way of being, and a new wave of living. The pods are landing now; there are a number of pods that hit the water.

The pods are travelling at high velocity but the pods are protected, they resemble a huge egg. It has numerous layers; it protects the cells from any radiation and anything that would cause them harm. All cells have been in the pods for over a decade now, and it feels safe for them to come out and explore. Some of the cells don't know where they will end up; all they know is that some of them are here at this new place.

This new world is where the cells begin a new life and put things to use as they see fit. This place is where they learn about original energy flow and learn to come together with their talents and prepare their new colonies.

The temperatures are dissimilar here on this strange planet; the cells are aware of the gauges in their pods and the frequencies of energy this planet holds. All the cells can perceive sound as well; they must find a sense of balance and a place that feels right and comfortable. The cell souls are searching through the old star maps, as cell souls they didn't imagine that they would be using the maps ever again.

The cells have touched ground on this new planet and can sense, then connect to the crystal grids. The crystals are very large and powerful, they are pointing the cells in a direction where they will be safe.

One of the pods hosts a family and their mission is for peace and abundance. The parents are Charmaine and George. George is not conscious yet for some reason. George has not fully awakened but he will soon. Charmaine see's that George isn't moving and is frightened; she can sense his energy from where she is standing in the pod.

Not knowing if her husband would come to grip with the sudden changes and new development of this new world. It is through Charmaine's feminine energy; she will become accustomed to this new earth and support him as George assists her through his male energy. Then they both can transmit the energy of balance together, so that they can be spiritually powerful.

They have one small child, he is just awaking now, he is alert and very proud of who he is becoming. Their son's telekinetic energy is rapid, and he is even tempered when using his abilities, his name is Sly. He is winking and touching his eyes. Charmaine can sense her son is tuning into his telepathic energies. She is noticing how Sly is welcoming her and his father through his vibrational energy.

Charmaine recognizes Sly is eager to see where the other pods have landed. He knows everyone has landed in a different place, and everyone will come together and meet; later. All the pods do not have calendars or access to time, as they remember from the old earth. The cells have knowledge and carry the experiences that will help them at the present.

The cell souls have space, freedom and a large amount of time to do countless things. The pods are slowing down now; the cell souls must prepare and brace themselves for when the pods stop. The pods are screeching and making earsplitting noises. The families know when the pods land and stop that they are out of harm's way and they can proceed to open the door above them.

The doors in the pods have been sealed for a long time; they all have diverse buttons and sensors that each family can handle. The cell souls in each pod can still employ their telepathic energies to open the latch. Charmaine notices George arousing, and he is saying to her telepathically, he is feeling exhausted. Charmaine mentions to Sly that they must plug his father into the generator and recharge his energy.

The generators on each pod have a hose that connects to each cell souls' new skin. The generator helps George and others to experience and connect to their new energy and vibration. It strengthens George through his heart and respiratory, which supports him through his breathing.

Charmaine and Sly observe George's colors' going from purple, dark blue, red and yellow.

Then the vibrations of color begin to balance out George's skin, to a soft yellow and green, then to a aqua. Sly and Charmaine sense George through his breathing, as they all experience each other's energy through their group breathing. The energy is felt first through their heart center, as they all acknowledge their chakras.

When the energy feels reasonable, then there is balance and the energy is strong. The cells will all bond and be familiar with this action. When balance is achieved within that second the hose will automatically disconnect. The families will stay in their pods regularly to replenish themselves, to sleep and rest, until they are assured what's outside.

The cell souls choose to do this, so they can achieve something in the new world. Until the cells outgrow the pods, they are their homes on this planet, the cells call her StarDrome, and she was once a merciless planet. There has been much rot, many battles, but StarDrome is healing. She is curing herself, the stronger her energies the healthier StarDrome feels. She is alive; the cells can feel her as they join her.

StarDrome recognizes the cells are there in a reasonable way, to bring new expansion. To carry joys, no discomforts in energy but the calm. StarDrome is the egg, the cells are in center, and it is akin to being in her womb. She is the mother and the cells will honor her and protect her, as she keeps them safe. StarDrome will point the cells in the right direction and guide them. Therefore they can learn to cultivate the land with her help.

The cells can learn to use and not take, to set balance with all energy on StarDrome. It is a good place and it feels right and the cells all believe they are exceptional here. There's a welcoming of energy from StarDrome and the door is opening to her core. The cell souls can hear the noise StarDrome makes and can articulate that the doorway to the new world, has been sealed for an extended time.

There is this deafening whooshing sound and a great discharge of energy, with a gust of cool gentle wind. StarDrome is welcoming the cells; as new seeds, they feel safe in their pods as they land. The cell souls have not sensed this energy and breeze for some time. As long as the gust of air doesn't turn their skin a different color, the cells know they are safe.

The cell souls created their own masks, these unique masks are worn over their face. The cells secure their masks from the tip of their nose, downwards, underneath their eyes, and around their ears. The ears of a cell soul are sensitive because this is how they breathe, from behind the ears. They are like amphibians, made particularly to go into the water and on land.

It is imperative for the cells to protect their skin, from the collarbone area to the top of their ears. Their breathing is vital on StarDrome so they are linking to this element of energy and identifying with it, so that the energy is acceptable. They can filter their energy now from the old earth.

Therefore, on StarDrome the cells can be parallel to the energy and attach to it through their heart, through all their senses. StarDrome is a living, breathing entity, just like the cells, but in a diverse way. Sly jumps up and down, he is excited, as the latch opens to their pod. Sly has shape-shifted into a spider, it is his defense. Sly is strong and willing to go outside on StarDrome and observe what this new world brings.

Sly is ahead of his parents leaving the pod and his father George follows and shape-shifts into a lion. He chooses to walk on his two legs, it is his protection. He has a shield to protect him and others, plus George has a sword. Charmaine starts shape-shifting into a phoenix; she is long and has a color of golden red. She is beautiful, aligned and well-built. The energy permeates from her heart, and she fly's outside the door and they proceed to situate themselves on top of the pod.

They start looking around and it felt so desolate there; but they recognized this is the place where they can start to establish themselves, with the other cells that arrived also. They have certain provisions that they set aside, this includes goods prepared beforehand, and that will aid them on this new planet.

The cells have water, food, and the necessities that will maintain them, until the pods shrink. This will determine their existence and life-force. The pods will last for a year; Charmaine and George remember those times on old earth, before StarDrome. A year may appear long, but it goes by rapidly. There are many requirements that each family must fulfill inside a few months, to be established on StarDrome.

The days continue to be long and the nights are diminutive. The cell souls know they have two to four hours of night. When they all utter night, it is pitch black with blue crystal energy. But these blue crystal energies are unsafe, it is good to distinguish these effects telepathically, because the cells know what they need to do to stay safe; and build their homes.

The day would be best, due to the brightness because these blue crystal energies can cause damage to their skin. The knife-like energy can generate a fire and rip through their skin (suit) and then their body takes on all toxins.

Then and there the bodies of the cells would be open to incredible and extreme damage. There would be no time to refurbish their suit once the harm is done. The body cannot reconstruct itself once those toxins enter. The energy of the toxins create venomous gases, it would not be good because the body will explode.

Other souls, who arrived on StarDrome, must be familiar with these things. Sly's family starts receiving messages from other families that have landed on the north side of StarDrome. The other cells are telepathically sharing information about the red and yellow balls of light, as they are dangerous, "Do not touch those things, under any circumstance".

Do not look at these things either, because you will be blinded. You will not see or hear these things coming, as they hide behind the trees". The trees on StarDrome aren't like the ones from old earth. These trees look more like cactus, but with arms and feet. Those balls of energy can hide behind those cacti and within them as well. The energy balls can give the impression of being like the roots of a tree.

The balls of energy can camouflage themselves quite adequately. But everyone on StarDrome must be cautious and discern with these effects, and Sly's family thanked the other cells for sharing from the north. Then Sly's family sent out telepathic messages to other cell families to warn them of the dangers on StarDrome.

Now the families must gather their supplies and find soil they can build on. Everyone first must agree to where they will take up residence. To find a special place on StarDrome where they can start to assemble, they must first set their energy points. The points are similar with a star; the cells must align their energies, to bring balance to the center of those points.

The star maps are connected to these five points and the energy frequencies radiant outwards from these points into the star system connecting with the other planets. The energy is a radio frequency for the other cells to connect with telepathically. Within these specific points of energy, the cells will construct their dwellings in the center; and this is how the cells stay safe. The center has four circles of energy and this helps the cells with their telekinesis.

The cell souls carry light lasers that facilitate the breaking of the ground, because they must go deep into the surface. Sometimes it is through very solid rock, but the cells must be careful not to harm the crystals. The circles of energy must be smooth, very soft. If they're not smooth, then they'll release toxins, gases, so a laser is perfect to cut into StarDrome's ground.

It's imperative that the cell souls know how to use the lasers because each cell studied extensively. If one does not know how to use the lasers it may perhaps create countless difficulties, this will cause problems in the breathing for any of the cells on StarDrome.

Those four circles must be completed in energy first, and then the star's points in each direction are set after that. Within the energy of those points, the star souls will protect the cells on StarDrome. This is where the cells could build their shields. The shields represent the doorways and they can travel in and out of any doorways; any time they choose.

The cells could also visit with other cells that landed on StarDrome safely with their pods as well; however they could only travel in and out of those doorways to visit each other. The shields are long tunnels of energy and the cells are protected as they travel back and forth at high velocity.

But the tunnels aren't ready yet, it will take a few days to construct. This will be the cells souls' transportation through these doorways and then they have the ability to carry the tools needed to assist each other. This way, the cell souls can assist each other with the resources they each hold individually.

On StarDrome the cells noticed; they don't need to walk to move around. The cells can raise their vibrations to lift themselves off the ground and float. Each different pod family has a distinct job to seize and take care of; for Sly's family it is the Spirit of the Water.

Sly is destined to take care of the discovery and the purifying of the water. Therefore, the water will be suitable for consumption and for other purposes on StarDrome. The water is diverse for the adult cells and for the children. The Spirit of the Water is altered as well for the cells that are still approaching StarDrome.

For the new star seeds they require a higher frequency of water, the energy vibrations in the water will assist the new souls that are coming to StarDrome. Vibration is the essence to all that is on StarDrome. The Lords are 'old souls', wise star-lights that carry all wisdom for every cell on StarDrome; through the Akashic records.

The Akashic records confirm to the cells presently, their intentions through time, up to this point. The intentions are connected to the old earth lessons, before the adult cells left the old earth. As a result they will be able to access these records and view them when they like, keeping up to date with all of the cells, and what they are doing, as they grow.

That is why the masters prohibit the use of old energy on StarDrome, the energy will create sickness and StarDrome will rid herself of anything old. In addition the records gift wisdom; teaching and guiding the cell souls about where they are going, and how they are creating destiny on StarDrome.

Through those records as cell souls, they are manifesting the best of the best intention. The teachings are very important to all cell souls on StarDrome. There are diverse teachers for different teaching effects in energy and the children must be mentors with them now.

Charmaine's son Sly and other cells from different pods, are unique individuals and will come together and learn from each other; and some of the children they teach are rainbow. Any cell could tell the rainbow by their colors which are orange, green and yellow. Some advanced rainbow children carry extra red, blue or white colors.

These colors sit from the base of their back up to the top of their head. To perceive these colors are imperative, to be able to recognize which ones are the rainbows. The rainbow children look unusual, and they have mentors set aside to support them.

Many of the rainbows are working with the elements and the grids, they encompass certain energies. They have been working with these energies before they came back to StarDrome again. Their insights and vision are incredibly clear, extremely in-depth. They can move belongings and shift equipment through their telekinesis energies exceptionally quick.

Some of the old souls on StarDrome are crystal children; any of the cells would be able to tell by the three crystals that meet at the top of their heads. There is a main crystal that positions itself at the base of their neck and this is their brain stem. If pulled out or moved in anyway it could bring instant death to the soul.

Each crystal represents something special in their growth, through their knowledge. Some of these crystals are blue, pink and some are red; a number of them are purple. The male crystal children have the purple and the females have the red. The children that have the strongest energies and colors are the ones that are tailored to meet StarDromes' demands.

The children carry the DNA of the star system and are wise beyond their years. These crystal children also sit in the points of the star, to protect StarDrome from any outside interference from other surrounding planets. These gifts strengthen the character of each one of them differently.

They will also facilitate and teach the smaller children, then eventually grow to replace the actual parents and guardians. They will start learning as early as two or three years old, which is aged for a soul. On StarDrome, the planet also includes the star warriors. There aren't many of them left to teach the cells, as they have perished and died off through the galaxy wars.

StarDrome has several star warriors left. She has at least eight and there are only two females within these star warrior groups. It is significant for the female warriors to teach the male warriors about their balance; between female and male energy. Then they can create with ease and then become our soldiers for peace.

The star warriors protect the crystal and rainbow children, the warriors are being trained to teach peace, not war as there has been too much war and decay through time. They sit in the classrooms for long periods of time, learning many things. They do not grow exhausted as they remember through their once human nature, but the star warriors shift through energy very rapidly.

Then the warriors travel to the libraries, where they can walk through the halls to the Akashic records; and obtain whatever it is that they need, as the Lords trust them. Then the knowledge from the records supports them, so that they see lucid and hear clear, then set balance within their systems (bodies) through their wisdom.

When the masters look at them through their visions, they can see through all veils behind them, they see the old ancients and gold beings working with them. The ancestors are there to support them telepathically so they can heighten their energy vibrations.

Not just through their telekinesis energies but it is through the records the warriors must study and learn. Subsequently they will see their big record books in front of them, as cell souls; they all have different piles of records to sort through. Diverse colors, similar degrees of energy to work through and read with speed and accuracy.

StarDrome has three ultimate beings of White Light to support them. These beings of White Light travel wherever they oblige themselves to travel, very swiftly. But they chose to travel to the other cell souls that have occupied different planets. These superlative beings can go anywhere because of their white light, it is seen through the skies.

These beings can repair the damage that was done, inside the energetic fields. These White Lights create the harmony that is needed, also, to sustain all cell souls on StarDrome, as the white light is the strongest energy field. You can witness the repairing of energy that is taking place through the galaxies and planets; everything must shift to a healthier place of balance.

There is a quantity of holes in the Milky Way where the White Lights are repairing the energetic fields. StarDrome has many recruits, supporting the Light Beings as the balance of StarDrome is of immeasurable importance.

Nearby you can notice countless effects of healing energy accumulating to aid them; they will be there for some time. As other souls grow they can be recruited if they choose and replace the recruits that have been there for some time, until the old recruits are ready to come back to StarDrome.

Each singular cell (soul) has a different purpose. Each different (cell) can shape-shift into what they discern as their strength and power. Some of the cell souls have two or three energy effects that they can shape-shift into. It depends on what each cell soul is directed to do, by their masters or mentors.

All the cell souls have this policy on StarDrome to keep peace. To constantly carry the (weak cells) who are still learning because some cell souls are young. Whatever needs to be discussed by the masters and mentors within that circle stays in that circle. This is where the sacredness exists and all truth stays within that circle.

We as the new inhabitants of StarDrome; are loved by our families and colleagues and the one's passed over; through all wisdom that is expressed together at this time; on this planet. We can choose to call it magic; some souls on old earth will fear that word. Others will observe it as a long tenuous journey again, depending on their awareness. It depends on the cells to how much they carry in responsibility and remembrance.

Some cell souls are still distraught and at a standstill because they still sense the earth energies from before, the devastation. The heartaches and sorrow that took place on old earth were tremendous for the families. Countless souls had to rise above the energy of the old vibrations, of old earth.

Many souls departed and had a choice to leave old earth, plus everyone knew of the changes coming and was forewarned. The old earth must refurbish itself now, at hand; there are still many inhabitants that are still on that planet. This was by choice, plus many couldn't raise their vibrations to match StarDrome's frequency.

Those people on old earth are dying slowly and are reclaiming their energies and power. Choosing to shift out of their weaknesses and vulnerabilities, and still dump the old energy of blame, shame, hate and denial.

The sacrifice and conditions that created war, disease and sickness. As cell souls we can still view those energies telepathically, on our screens. The screens are in front of each cell soul. They can notice the screens automatically, when tuning in to the energy, by looking visually.

Some cell souls have larger screens, so they can glimpse into several things, at one time. The cells can focus their energy to witness more or less, depending on the frequencies of what they require. How they learn from their screens, depends on each cell soul's awareness.

The cells always have access to the old earth behaviors through their screens. Then, as mentors and masters they can teach the young souls and the new souls; coming to StarDrome. Then the young souls can learn to keep the energy that is positive, and build on that frequency on StarDrome.

When all cell souls, lay their hands on the ground of StarDrome, they must focus their energy to bring her to life. The cell souls must experience the heart of that land, which is the energy of StarDrome.

Afterward the cells can let StarDrome know they are there in peace, in a good way. At that point the cells would be honored onto this new land to grow, as StarDrome propagates with them. Then the cell souls can proceed to create harmony, peace and demonstrate to this new earth their visions.

There is a great amount of faith given from the cells; that they perceive and bring together positive flow. Without disease, sickness, and death, here on this planet, as cells they can create new beginnings. Through their highest frequencies of energy, that each cell can give; while on StarDrome.

Then they can truly love, laugh and live again. Until each cell fulfills their new vibrations on StarDrome; and with each other. After that, each cell can see the vibrations of amazing energy surround them and protect them, through the galaxies.

StarDrome, the new world is ready; she is accepting all cell souls now; because they are tuned into her energy and life-force. First through their feet and then StarDrome connects and aligns with them individually through their energy systems.

From side to side the veins of StarDrome enlighten their bodies and energy, which is the powerhouse of StarDrome. The energy of StarDrome is felt through their feet, to the tops of their heads. The energy is transmuted through their wings, and then the cell souls stretch their wings out to each other, so they can reach (different colored energy places on StarDrome.)

Now, the cells connect with the other wings; of the soul families. Even within other pods, to unite their energies and frequencies, so they are equivalent to each other.

Their visions and inspirations facilitate each cell, to transmute love and light energy all the time.

The cells are healing naturally through their energies with StarDrome. The energy recharges everything on StarDrome, in all directions. As the cells look around they can see the spheres of energy, as it unites.

While they sit within their energy frequencies of spirit, the cells can see, feel and hear the energy of StarDrome come to life. All the forces of energy connect with light and passion. Every cell family can feel the heart energy explode and send healing rays of light to StarDrome and her new inhabitants.

The cell souls create through their dreams and are lending their gifts to promote each other's energy on StarDrome. The cell souls appreciate each other's pictures and visions of what they are going to create, on this magnificent planet.

If, they stand tall with spirit, they can align with StarDromes' (pictures, duties, and ballads).

As cells, they can feel the potency of energy through their hearts; the cells are building up an immense energy that connects to all hearts on StarDrome. While they align their new energy, the vibration starts to break open the terrain.

Currently StarDrome is feeling loved, caressed and a renewal of hope. The empowerment through all energies on StarDrome can be felt to its full potential. StarDrome is now aware she will be nurtured and loved, right down to her rocks.

StarDrome starts to shake, move and create more energy. The energy is a smooth beam of light that creates this break in the planet's crust. As StarDrome opens her doorways in the north, she is creating new ground and steps. The additional stones and sand of StarDrome start to settle down, where the cells first landed their pods.

The cells can sense all the offspring shape-shift into their power, and then the youngsters dance and walk on a new ground. The children call the new ground of StarDrome, their playground.

They can detect the fairies, the water ponds and warm summer scents, as StarDrome creates new with them. The summer fish and a lone starfish, there is a great deal of beauty on StarDrome. All cells honor this beauty through their essence of energy and through all their special colors and frequencies of light.

Then all the cell souls reached their arms out into the universe and celebrated with the energies of their new home. The cells choose to create a new life-force, and the energy will strengthen and harmonize StarDrome. The energy of each other helps them to develop telepathically and aids them in the alignment process.

This way, as cell souls, they can connect to everything that is energy on this planet. The kids are laughing, smiling and singing "ring around the energy" - they experience the energy of blue, purple and green, with bits of red. The joy and happiness is felt through the playful energies of the innocent.

Some of the cells were once victims through the ages passed down to all of them; as cell souls. The energy of creation has come to be successful, through peace.

Every cell can witness some green healing energy coming out of the ground where they thought plant life wouldn't grow.

Plant life now grows between the rocks; the cells have new growth on StarDrome. The cell souls have done a lot of energy work, but they must retire and go back to their pods until tomorrow. The temperatures are cooling down very quickly on StarDrome; this temperature will freeze their skin, so the cells must enter the pods immediately.

They sent each other telepathic messages, so they all could return back to their safe havens within their pods. All the cells need to make sure that the door and the latch to their pods are sealed properly; so that nothing can get in, because apparently those little red balls of energy can squeeze into anything.

Those red energy balls can camouflage themselves, because there's a foreign creature inside each ball that likes to create harm and anxiety to its victims. The cells will study its habits one day, but this alien creature wishes to pull out all the plugs through the systems within each pod.

This way the cells won't produce any negativity with anything on StarDrome and risk the chances of decaying. The night is coming fast, the cells must go now. At this time, most of the cells can feel the tips of their ears freezing.

All of the cell soul's must shape-shift back into their skin (body) that they have. Some of them have skin that is green with blue twinges, and others' have golden specks of energy running through their wings. The wings can reverse into their backs, when needed as they shape shift.

All of the cells make sure that they remind each other telepathically, to seal the door to their pods; each pod matches their type of energy. This is how each cell family knows who is housed where, as cell souls they were taught how to observe the energy around the latch.

As it closes and seals itself, to be certain the pods are safe, again for the night. The hours of darkness will appear long, even though it is only four hours, but seems like eight or ten. Now, the cells will need to eat, so they adjust the tubes that are plugged into the holes in their lower backs.

All of the cell souls have hoses in their pods, filled with red energy; they are nurtured with food from these hoses. Each hose is different for each cell soul and family. The hoses will sustain them until each cell soul grows out of the pods; and then the ground of StarDrome will be fertilized with new growth.

The cells need to produce the things that will sustain them on StarDrome, as all the cells have a different mission. The cells have hoses in each different pod, that works quickly, within a few seconds, and then the cells are satisfied and full.

If only these things were on old earth, maybe then there would have been no fighting etc.; all the cells are full and content, and they can feel their energy of fullness through their sacred breathing.

The cell souls can now rest; the pods are quiet and humming with softness. Sly is already tucked in his bed, George and Charmaine can sense him downloading the energies and records he needs now, so that he can do his dream work.

Sly's parents, they must do the same to strengthen their bodies (skins)" Until all the cell souls awaken, to gather again, in the next few hours…

Good night. (This can be heard telepathically, across StarDrome) StarDrome then settles her energy down for the night.

2

Sly Awakens

The journey begins

A year has passed on StarDrome; all the pods are disappearing and getting smaller; as all the cell souls have grown, who inhabitant the pods. Sly wakes up with a terrible headache and he is sweating profusely, not wanting to remember the last minutes he saw his parents alive. He still holds on to the energy of blame, and knows, if he would have just listened, things might have turned out differently.

Sly is aware he can't hold onto such human emotions on StarDrome, especially as a mentor. Sly thinks back (if only) his parents had a few seconds longer, to enter the pod, he knows his parents chose to go looking for him. Then his parents got caught in the night as they pushed Sly into the pod and then telepathically locked it.

Sly tries to shake the memories away and he knows that he has to leave his pod before long. Sly is out- growing the pod, it's becoming too tight and small, but he recognizes he's trying to keep his memories alive; by staying in the pod his family called home, as much as he can.

Sly must practice further his shape-shifting skills to stay alive. He doesn't wish to use his common name anymore; he feels that it's time to just carry his new name. Sly acknowledges that he is required as a mentor, to connect to the crystal and rainbow children that are learning and growing with their gifts very rapidly.

Sly acknowledges that he has taken some time out and was being extremely stubborn about doing anything. He knows at this time through his sadness and grief, that he can't hold that energy. The energy of sadness and grief is of low vibration and it will create disruption.

High vibrations of energy don't match low vibrations on StarDrome. Sly only felt that one person was close to him through his whole ordeal and transition. Sly knows that other cell souls have tried to console him it's just that he chose not to receive the aid.

Sly was eager to leave things alone and he chose to isolate himself. There has been new growth of vegetation on StarDrome and Sly isn't quite sure where he'd like to be in a year. But he knows that he has the qualities to work with water, very well; indeed.

The water spirits are alive in the water and they've been trying to get Sly's attention for some time. Sly tries to ignore the water beings and attempts to shrug that energy of awareness off. But, Sly knows that it's time to do what he came to do on StarDrome, it is to mentor.

Now, Sly will choose to call himself Spider Boy, through this energy Sly is protected. This new spider energy is Sly's shell and it's getting stronger as he learns about his gifts. Sly is aware he carries poisons as Spider Boy, to protect himself and he notices that he has very strong antennas. (That's what Sly refers to them, as).

The very things that help him tune in to energy frequency and become aware of all his surroundings. Sly wasn't really thrilled at first to shape shift into a spider but it took some getting use too. There are numerous waves of energy that Spider Boy is sending out in his thoughts, in the moment, he must remind himself to be more diligent.

Sly remembers to test his armor, when he shape-shifts each day into a spider. Sly can feel the strength in his thick legs, develop daily. Especially the spot of green energy on the side of his right leg, it's very solid. It's a strange spot but has superior senses and strong energy.

Sly's senses are improving more each day; he can smell from miles away. Sly knows when he needs to put up his shields on both sides of his shell, as he can sense strange things entering his space (aura) or if he is in harm's way.

Sly has strong sensors to heat and cold temperatures, and recognized that he can't really climb when it's cold. Sly realizes that a lot of the other parents have died off, and he starts to question if this is the way it was meant to be.

Sly wonders if all the children including him are left to fend for themselves and continue as shape-shifters. Sly knows, as a cell soul that he and others can't stay in these pods anymore. These pods won't hold their fast growing bodies anymore.

Many of the cell souls are growing fast and shape shift at rapid speed. Through all that growth, their telepathic and telekinesis energies are increasing and growing resilient. Sly knows that he wants to use his gifts for good, but Sly also acknowledges that he has his gifts for battle too, in case of negative intrusion.

Master Silver Cloud mentioned there was a possibility of old folks coming to StarDrome, as the old earth is depleting. But he knew that they didn't have the resources to build a craft to take them here, to the new world. Maybe one day something goes bad or becomes rough and out of hand…

Spider Boy then checks the sensors on his left foot; they don't feel as strong as they did when he was shape-shifting. But he's aware of them and knows that the sensors are there. Sly now feels better as a spider, faster, more alert. Sly knows that he's getting hungry and he's got to go and get food, as he can't use the hose's anymore.

Then he automatically thinks of a spider and what they eat... it wasn't a good picture, he saw in his visions. Sly realizes he must eat before he shape shifts; it's easier because he doesn't sense he could eat flies. Now, Sly acknowledges that the pods are shrinking and he's growing fast, even for a spider.

It's about coming together with other cell souls and doing some work and sharing the labor. We were taught by Master Shade, nothing is labor and any energy is to be appreciated.

Sly proceeds to meet his friend Luna in that day, he tries not to send his telepathic thoughts to her. Because Sly's thoughts are energy of 'like' towards Luna, a deep energy of fondness.

The masters know, as Sly and Luna become older, Sly knows that they are destined to be together. Sly is positive that Luna is aware of this also, but can't be certain she knows. Both Luna and Sly pretend that they don't know anything, but it is awkward because they are both aware of this circumstance since birth.

Sly shakes his head to let go of any thoughts as he walks towards Luna. She then shape shifts into a beautiful, stunning pony. Sly knows as Luna gets older she'll mature into a beautiful horse. Sly notices that Luna has beautiful red, auburn hair that catches the light at the right time. Luna has such strength and agility already.

Luna has such grace at the same time, it mesmerizes Spider Boy. Sly tries not to be bashful, thinking about Luna, as he is aware that she'll pick up his telepathic messages. Sly's not certain what Luna might think, but Sly knows Luna is excellent at holding her energy and thoughts at low key.

This then keeps Sly on his toes, to know that Luna is aware of his every thought. Luna has deep blue eyes, similar to the ocean. Sly knows that he can get lost in Luna's eyes easily. Sly wishes he could just take Luna away somewhere, someday.

Then they can both live somewhere else besides StarDrome... he would take good care of her. But they're too young now, they're only twelve and thirteen years old, but in star years they're over 100. Luna and Sly still carry the same blueprints, as they've done before, in other journeys.

They have both travelled before in other distances and they only take the things in energy they need to sustain them. Presently, on StarDrome all cell souls are learning additional things on how to grow vegetation and what they can't grow on StarDrome.

Sly realizes in the present day, while visiting Luna on the eve of his mother's death, that he must leave his pod now. Sly knows through his mother's spirit, that she will strengthen him and keep him on track so he keeps his faith. Now that he finished visiting with Luna, Sly must go back to his pod now and gather the things that he needs.

As some of the cell souls do the same, because they also recognize their pods are shrinking too. Sly has his spear; it's made of titanium and he knows that it is the resilient metal, and the sword opens up on both sides, it's like two in one.

The sword also closes through one small opening on each side of the sword.

This blade is Sly's weapon of choice because Sly knows if he's not camouflaged as Spider Boy, he can't carry the sword in his hand. As Spider Boy, Sly must learn how to carry the sword and study it carefully to see if it could change into anything else.

Sly can practice with the sword by this time, at high swiftness, as he's trained for some period with his father. Sly has some war wounds to prove it, on his right side. He even has one scar that resembles a Rose, when he looks down at it. Some might think the scar looks like something else, but Sly knows what he perceives.

As, Spider Boy his scars are his merits, to others his scars might be just scars. The scars Sly received were for all the battles and lessons he endured as a warrior. No one knows he is a descendent from the Stars, as it is written in the Book of Truth.

Spider Boy has learnt and appreciates the lessons the elders are teaching. Sly knows he will learn through others, he'll have many gifts on his spiritual tool belt. Sly will choose to use these spiritual tools in honor, as he has vivid visions already.

With his telepathic gifts he will mentor others, because there are only a few teachers, with certain gifts and abilities. Sly is aware that he was chosen for a reason, to oversee the teachings of the younger ones, when it is time. Luna is also part of these teachings as a mentor; she has been learning many things as well.

Luna might not recognize that yet, but Sly knows that she's being prepared for something big. Luna's name is Swift One when she shape shifts into a beautiful horse. No one can catch her; she's akin to the wind. One minute Sly would see her in front of him, the next minute she is right beside him.

SpiderBoy will ride on Luna's back and connect to Luna's energy one day, when they are both older. But right now Sly desires to leave his thoughts where they should be, quietly behind him. Then he can focus on the tasks at hand, as he's still picking up supplies from his pod.

Sly can't let his mind wander or let his thoughts get in the way. Sly is learning to be disciplined in his thinking. Its discernment, so he doesn't think of Luna all the time. Spider Boy must stay focused, or Swift One will pick up on the telepathic messages he thinks.

Spider Boy has a lot of work ahead of him, as Luna could surprise him with her knowing and thoughts.

Spider Boy has everything he needs in supplies; he's keeping his thoughts on what he's doing. Sly is saying goodbye to his pod, his home.

He then gathers up his supplies, Sly notices in the middle of his right hand his sensor is vibrating and it sits about an inch from his wrist. All Sly has to do is press it once and hold it for a minute; this is how Sly realized he could zap the pod away. Sly looked at the pod in front of him and he noticed every time he held down his sensor; the pod becomes smaller and less significant until it's was gone.

Sly was amazed by what he just done and realizes his sensor has many uses. The only thing left from his family's pod was his silver spoon. Sly then proceeds to pick up the silver spoon and notices it has its own memory cells. Sly could see the violet colors in the spoon. Sly senses that he desires to put the silver spoon above his heart, in his pocket.

Then he will always hold the memories of his parents and home, just by holding the spoon. Now, Sly will continue his journey as a young man, destined for many things on StarDrome. Sly leaves the place he remembers as his home, the pod is gone but his memories are in the spoon.

Only Sly could read the energy and hear what the spoon is sharing with him. SpiderBoy must go forward to teach the young ones and learn from the old Ones. As all inhabitants grow and learn from each other on StarDrome. The cell souls are building and creating new homes and destinies.

On StarDrome the cells have an area of land they designated as a storage room; it has a huge ceiling of energy that goes from the north, east. The shields are big enough to protect them from any low vibrations of energy attack.

The cell souls also have a dome of energy that protects them and surrounds all of StarDrome; StarDrome has energy shields that can close over the dome any time. The shields reach out into the universe, as far as the cells like it to go, to keep all things safe through the galactic ancestors.

All the cell souls are housed in a cylinder of energy, a circular shape, it is vast expansive energy; but they can move and manipulate the energy as they grow.

The cell souls can choose to create the walls, rooms or space for storage or for their homes, any way they like. With their creative energy the cell souls can create the things they need, for studies and teaching others.

The cell souls have their own labs and designated area's set aside, where they teach others to swim and adapt to StarDrome. They also have teachers that are swimmers, from the old colonies on earth.

Some of the mentors work with the swimmers, such as whales, octopus and algae, there are many new arrivals, and some are so little. But everything plays a role on StarDrome; the teachings that need to take place are increasing every day.

Sometimes it seems like there isn't enough mentors and masters on StarDrome. SpiderBoy goes and collects his spiritual tools and puts them into his satchel. Then sly chose's to go down to the water so he can meditate and talk to the water spirits, about his new move.

Then the water spirits can share the wisdom for Sly's new direction on StarDrome. This is SpiderBoy's way of learning to listen to direction, so that he can seek guidance for whatever it is that he needs. Sly can see other youngsters learning from the water elements as well.

Sly notices at least four or five young cell souls, who are sitting in close proximity to him, in different positions. They're all meditating and watching what the elements are showing them, all individually. Spider Boy also recognizes that some of the young souls have a viewing screen.

The screen is about fourteen inches wide from top to bottom. The cell souls can view and learn from what's seen and heard on the screen, in front of them. It's also how they catalogue and keep track of the things they are learning. Sly notices he has a viewing screen also, it's on his left side. Everything needs to be tracked, to keep inventory on StarDrome, it's important because the lives of every cell soul matters.

The consumption of food and water was in excess on old earth. On StarDrome all cell souls are taught to honor what they use daily, by taking inventory of their supplies and usage. It keeps everyone organized because every cell has a different job to do on StarDrome.

29

The tasks complement each cell soul's 'gift of what they chose to give each other, to set balance on StarDrome. SpiderBoy quietly sits by the water and closes his eyes, then puts his three fingers from his right hand into the water, as directed from the water beings.

Sly takes a nice deep breath from inside out and telepathically asks the water to bring him the teachings that will help him connect deeply to the water's history. SpiderBoy first recognized all the wonderful colors of blue in the water that came to life in the center of his hand.

Then the blue energy starts to move up his arm, throughout his body. The energy then moves through his body at high speed, tickling and caressing him. Sly then sense's this deep profound sensation of love welcoming his energy, this comes from the water beings.

The water beings are telepathically speaking to Sly and directing him to look on his viewing screen. The water beings then continue to demonstrate to Sly what tasks are at hand, for him on this new planet. The time frames involved for each lesson is diverse for each soul.

The water beings are very energetic; these water beings love very deeply. Sly notices that their great teachers and he will need to pay close attention, not to miss out on anything that they have to share.

Many of the water beings are of different sizes and shapes; they are flowing in and out of Sly's head also. Through his space (aura) by keeping it clear and keeping him conscious, by assisting Sly get over his pain and his agony; mentally and emotionally.

All this unwanted energy has accumulated in Sly's head, back and face and the water beings are helping him clear and feel calm. The water beings are directing Sly to look at his screen so he can see that his mother is all right. Then

Sly senses that there are other beings in the distance, around him doing something else.

Sly tries to stop the picture on his screen but he can't, other beings of light are stronger than him. They want him to focus his intentions on the screen. Sly starts shifting in and out of meditation, the other children take notice that Sly is shape shifting to a Spider and then back to himself again.

But this action kept repeating for quite some time as they all watched. At that time Sly immediately takes his hand out of the water and it immediately stops the connection to the water beings. At that moment Sly notices that his screen went blank and then he proceeds to wipe the tears flowing from his eyes.

Sly realizes he lost his connections, he didn't know if he wanted to see how his mother is doing, he felt his emotions over whelm him. Sly was trying to be brave and strong and then he just broke down and cried the deepest howls from the depth of his gut.

Sly realized that he felt and seen so many things emotionally and he had to learn from the water beings to stay grounded. Sly knew he needed to let go and heal his emotions, the water beings were helping and supporting him to do this.

But sometimes it's hard to feel and see everything emotionally, mentally all at once, it takes practice daily. Sly watched the water beings jump from his fingers back into the water. Sly was amazed to see them jump up and down with laughter and glee.

Sly knew in that moment, the water beings helped and supported him in his healing. Sly lifts his head up and shifts it to the left, he sees the water beings helping others. So they can also move through their experiences, and assist the other cell souls too.

Sly gazes across the water, he takes notice that all the same and similar practices with the water beings are taking place, with the children. But Sly noticed that the teachings were special, knowing inside intuitively that the water beings were helping all of them.

Sly then senses the difference of energy in his heart and breathing, through his chest and respiratory. SpiderBoy acknowledges that he was given a gift, not just a prophecy. But with an inner knowing of comfort, free will and choice. Sly then feels content with these energies completely, while he holds these energies to his heart and breathes in the energy of love.

Sly discerns that he feels fine with everything, as he moves forward, into his journey. Sly is already aware he has a couple of children to mentor; he will be teaching them through the experiences he's gained. The young cell souls will be under his wing, they are a boy and a girl.

The young girl is about three, the boy is older, and they are both excited about their growth and the experience they will receive through Sly's teachings. SpiderBoy must introduce himself and welcome them into his space just outside, from where he stays in his dome of energy.

Sly decides to go and prepare the room for his studies and the things that he's going to be teaching the two younger children. The girl is a crystal child and the boy is a star child, the boy reminds Sly of himself, even though they're different.

Through their different molecular makeup they both resemble similar things, with very different characteristics. Sly can already see that the young boy has power, that he can shift shape into a panther. Sly notices that his student has not used his energy to shape shift yet, from what he can notice the panther is very powerful.

The panther's energy is strong as he is a healer, protector and hunter. Sly realizes that he must keep an eye on him, so that his student can make the transition and shape-shift gradually. As Sly's student connects to the energy of being a four-legged. Sly's female student likes to work with crystals and she is already showing Sly how she heals the birds.

Sly watches how his student can bring them back to life. Sly's student is also learning how not to use up her energy, until she empowers herself daily, then she can save more lives. But now Sly must teach her how to embrace her energy, so that she can become stronger and telepathic.

Sly recognizes that the female's energy is strong and quick, from what he can make out. Spider Boy feels good about that and the little girl is known as Samantha, people call her Sammie for short. Sly is bonding with both Sammie and Panther Struts, Sly acknowledges that he will work well with both of them and he comprehends that they will have fun as they shape-shift.

Sly's thoughts were heard out loud by both kids in that moment; 'very good until we meet again, Sly said. He motions to the young ones to go enjoy the day, as he is choosing to lie down and rest. Sly feels drained from all the emotional and mental energy he has been sensitive to lately.

Plus, he knows that when he wakes up in the morning he'll have lots of work to do with these kids. Sly is aware of the things he must teach his students and he knows that he will be educating himself, as he has teachers too.

Sly understands that he will learn from them as he's teaching the younger ones. Sly also remembers his parents saying something to him, 'we are all teachers to each other'. Then telepathically Sly sends love and light to all his friends on StarDrome and quietly mentions,' until we talk in the morning'.

Sly smiles and slowly closes his eyes and then suddenly looks around his space with one eye and then closed it. Sly felt safe and then he envisions the stars as he falls asleep...

3

Sly Mentors

Sammie and Justin

Sly rubs his temples and he feels this heavy weight on his chest and he's wondering if he is dreaming. Sly tries to tune into the energy and it feels familiar to him. Sly then hears this chuckle and it's followed by laughter, next Sly opens one eye and takes notice that Justin is jumping on him.

Sly stares at Justin and telepathically says,

"Justin, what are you doing?"

"Oh, I just needed to wake you up," Justin said. "You were sleeping in." After that Sly tunes into the energy of time, as StarDrome doesn't have clocks. Sly notices the time of day by the warmth or coolness of temperature in his room. Sometimes Sly feels the dampness and he knows it is not quite 7 am and he looks at Justin and says,

"Why are you waking me up before it's time for me to get up?" Suddenly, Justin stops jumping on Sly and with a bewildered look on his face Justin replies, "I was excited to learn from you today,"

Then Justin looks at Sly with a peculiar look on his face and Sly is grinning. "I understand, sly states. "Where is Sammie? She must be here, too." Just as Sly thought that, he can hear this crunching noise coming from his left side. At that moment Sly speaks to Justin quietly, "Yes, someone is eating before we even portion our food out."

As soon as Sly whispered that, he can hear these little tears and whimpering sounds coming from Sammie. Within that moment Sammie starts to cry and say, "I'm so sorry. I'm so sorry. I was hungry and I needed to put something in my tummy. I don't know where my mommy is and I needed something to eat or else I don't feel good." Sammie explained;

At that point Justin jumps down off Sly's chest and he runs over and hugs Sammie so that she feels better.

"It's OK, Sammie. It's OK. You have me now, I'm here to protect you and watch over you." Justin sturdily said; then Sly yawns and he looks at both of the kids and he declares, "Well, I guess I can get up now.

We have a long day ahead of us, as you are my little students. I was once learning these things too and healing my emotions, it's Ok! Let's just pick this food up, let's portion it out properly because it needs to last us throughout the day, Sly explained.

I need to go and collect certain tools to help us tomorrow. There are some tools that I need to take into this healing room where we're going to be learning, Sly said. So let's just make sure that you both are feeling good and comfortable and then we can get ready for what we need to do.

Sly said with a smile; please make sure that you both drink lots of water, we have good water, as I work with the water beings. The water beings have blessed us with good health and the water will help us purify our cells.

This is good to remember through our breathing exercises we can create relaxing energies in our bodies, we need to be doing these exercises before we start and when we finish our sessions'.

Sly then proceeds with their morning and he indicates not to make it a long day, but he chooses to introduce longer periods to the kids each day as a new day. The time fly's by for Sly as he is teaching and working with his students, Justin and Sammie.

"It already feels like it's been a long day," Justin says, but I'm getting hungry. "And we can't really cook anything the way we used to." Justin tunes in telepathically on StarDrome to see whose cooking.

There are one or two mentors over in the North, eating and getting ready with the children they teach. Therefore, Sly's students take a break and come back tomorrow, so they can continue learning from Sly.

The first day was easy for all of them until they meet again in the morning. This time Sly made sure that Justin understood, 'no jumping on my body', to wake me up. The night went by slowly and all was good until the next day, Sly awakes to work with the students.

Sly had a full day organized as the masters insisted that many things get done, especially if StarDrome was going to grow. Sly mention's to his students that they are both doing a great job and he is proud of them both.

It was still early in the morning when the sun was rising and Justin walks up to Sly; "Oh this isn't so bad," Justin pronounces. "Well," said Sly. "No, it's pretty good. We've got one or two people who are awake this morning.

This is good and he proceeds to thank Justin for waking him up. Then Sly mentions to the children that it is crucial that everyone keeps busy on StarDrome, as the masters insisted for many reasons.

Sly notices that Sammie looks pretty good, and she's all ready to learn, but then Sly is wondering to himself, 'well, how am I going to get that little bear away from her arms? She's holding on to it pretty tight. Plus, Sly is aware that Sammie needs to choose to set it aside, while she is learning.

At that moment Sly had an epiphany and thinks to himself, 'I can somehow include her bear in these exercises', I'm teaching. The masters would be okay with that, as long as it wasn't impeding on the lessons. Sly smiles to himself; subsequently as Sly thought that, he had to remind himself to remember his thoughts.

All of a sudden, Sammie said to him. "As a matter of fact, it's ok' Sly, I can put Davie on the floor beside me." Then Sammie smiled the biggest smile and hugged Sly's leg. Sly was quite surprised; Sammie read and heard his thoughts quite clearly.

"Oh yes, you're correct." Sly thought .That was your first lesson, the telepathic messages." Then Sly grinned at Sammie and said, Thank you! Sly glanced over to Justin, he could see Justin grinning from ear to ear, and he says to Sammie: "I told you, he hears, Justin knows what he's doing too.

Justin telepathically mentions to Sammie, 'Sly is a great teacher," Then Justin proceeds to put his arm around Sammie and then they both proceeded to follow Sly to the healing room. Sly adores the healing room; it's a little bit different than the one he studies in with the masters.

Sly refers to this room, he teaches in, as his learning room. Because it has golden rays flowing around the room and it's a strong vibration of energy. But once Sly or anyone goes into that room they can change the vibration and colors of energy, to match what their teaching or learning.

All cell souls can work with energy they harness, in that moment. Sometimes the cell soul can start off at a very small vibration, as the energy frequencies travel at different speeds. This way it's not too fast or too quick for certain cell souls, "Because they're little and still new at reining their energy."

Plus Sammie agreed with that thought. Next, Justin got excited as he ran into the room and just as he did that, Justin remembered: "I need to ask permission before I come into this sacred space." Then Justin quietly backs up until he's at the door again and he telepathically asks, "Can I come in please?"

Sly takes notice and smiles, and then all of a sudden, they all hear a loud stern voice in their ears. This is what they all heard, "Yes, do come in. Make yourself at home." Justin took a big breath inward and he went inside first.

Justin telepathically said, that this is his favorite sacred space; and he then proceeds to find the spot he loves to sit in. Justin then positions his body comfortably as he chose's the left side of the room.

Justin starts to look around and notices that there's not much stuff in this room, and it has changing colors of energy flowing through it. Justin continues to relax and get into a meditative state, and then he sees that Sammie is doing the same.

Justin takes notice that Sammie is just smiling and she's quite content, and she even left Davie at the door. He was surprised that Sammie did that, but he also noticed that Sammie is holding something else in her hands. Sly turns and sees that Sammie chose to sit in the middle of the room, and then she looked up at Justin and telepathically said; "I'm a big girl now." she smiled and then prepared herself comfortably on the floor.

But on StarDrome the ground was full of rocks and dust, the cells created soft green grass. The softest that you'd ever touch, that's just the way Sammie likes it. In that moment Sly sensed the energy of Sammie's expression. Sly knew intuitively, it was going to be a special day.

Sammie and Justin were sitting on the ground quietly meditating, while waiting for Sly to prepare. Both Sammie and Justin felt and seen how big Sly's energy can get, as he focused his energy all over the room, to hold the space. Then Sly disappeared and his energy encompassed the room.

Sammie and Justin knew it was Sly, because they saw him come into the room. They both witnessed Sly's energy at work and how he connected to everything. Sammie could see the purples, greens and blues in Sly's energy. Justin was just trying to touch and grab out to the energy, as he telepathically said hi to Sly: "I can see you there!"

The energy just moved and danced around Sammie and Justin. The energy was positioning them in a good place, so that they both feel comfortable. This way, Sly knew both Sammie and Justin would sense good things about what they're learning.

All of a sudden both students' could feel the energy on the top of their heads, and both Sammie and Justin chuckled because the energy tickled them. Sly could feel that both his students were letting him know, it's safe and clear to learn, now. By this time, both Sammie and Justin could sense the energy wrap around them.

They noticed that the energy was trying to show them something through their visions. Directly in front of Sammie and Justin, there was this energy board, and the board holds all this different kind of magical energy. All of a sudden a magical pencil appears beside each board, the pencils are all white and flawless.

The pencils are a little wider than your regular pencils that they remember Master Shade showing them; from the old world. "But it's still a pencil," Sammie declares telepathically.

Her pencil had a pinkish type of energy at the top of it, and Justin's pencil was green, with a hue of blue that sits in the middle of it. "And these pencils are the ones we are both going to use on these boards, right;" Justin said noisily.

"Well, they're not real blackboards," thought Sammie. "But it's a good...then Sammie stops talking, and then she looks at the pencil and board for a while. Because; remember she's just three. So, then they are both reminded to breathe again, and then Sly connects to his body and grounds his energy, to remain present for his students.

Sly takes all his energy back to his center and then the kids' notice his energy is peeling off the walls. They both witnessed Sly's energy come back into his aura and how the energy was making this imprint of him, in the room. Then the energy starts to reside and settle down around Sly; and make an imprint of him as a spider.

Sammie and Justin were surprised, how big this spider was, "Wow", said Sammie and Justin together.

"Ah, yes. That felt really cool;" Sly said, with a very big grin. Sly felt captivated by his energy and the things he did in this room. He sends this telepathic message into the universe, and he pronounces, "I feel bigger than life." There is this expansion of energy through joy, love and gratitude.

Everyone could feel it in the room, and then Sly lets the universe know that he loves teaching the children. Sly knew deep down inside, that he was at the right place at the right time doing what he came to do: teach.

Sly acknowledged being a mentor, and that these children would grow and learn to take the positivity out of every situation. Sly felt he would also benefit from both of them, as Sly knew that they all learn from each other. Observing both Sammie and Justin, as he sat with his legs crossed, he then said to the children, in a nice stern voice, "Let's start"!

Take those pencils that you have, and draw whatever you want, on that canvas in front of you. Create and see what colors' come to life on your boards." Both kids seem a little despondent, and then Sly telepathically said to them, "Ok, I will start."

Sly gets his board out, and he knew exactly where to find it. He had two helpers that were helping him. They were pixies. Sly enjoyed working with his little helpers and his board, as he referred to it as his canvas. The kids could call it a board and Sly just wants to show them how to be more creative with the resources around them.

Sly's helpers were both unique and always getting into some kind of mischief, then Sly said, "Create and draw the first thing that pops into your mind "draw a picture of it on your board, using any color or shape."

Spider Boy is watching the children bring the energy of this board to life. Then Spider Boy watches the energy of the canvas, turn into a multitude of colors' and different shapes. Sly observes the energy on both boards, while the energy shifts in and out of each board, with the pixies help. He notice's the energy on Justin's board turn red and white, it kind of reminded Sly of the candy canes from the old earth; the ones Master Shade gave them.

"Hmmm, haven't seen those for a long time", Sly utters. As they all continued working with their magical energies, and colors on their boards. Everything the kids were drawing on their boards, started coming to life, on its own. Justin is creating these wonderful beautiful masterpieces, and Sly can see how creative Justin is becoming.

Sly knew deep down inside, that he had the greatest students, as he watched them create magic. Suddenly, Sly recognized an energy come to life on Justin's board, it was his panther energy. "Hmmm," Sly says' to himself, he didn't say anything to Justin;

He just chose to appreciate how much Justin was aware, through his own energy. Because, Sly knew panther was a powerful symbol. Sly then quietly looks over at Sammie and notices that she's got the sun in the center of her board. Sammie is drawing all her energy from the sun, and maybe has two stars there as well.

Sly knows the sun is a very interesting symbol and then he asks Sammie why she drew a sun, she said, "Because it keeps me warm. Then Sly says, "Well that's not too bad, it would probably keep me warm, too." And he smiles;

At that point he says to Sammie, "What else do you sense or see in your board?

What do the stars represent Sammie?" At that moment Sammie rubbed her head, and saw her stars and then looked at Sly, and then glanced at Justin, and telepathically said, "One star is like home." Then she sighs.

"Interesting," said Sly. "What about the other star?" Sammie viewed the other star on her board and she whispered, "That star is my mom."

Everything went quiet and Sly could see and sense the energy of fear and sadness that Sammie felt in that moment. Sammie started to explain that she didn't mean to say, what she had said. Justin was looking at Sly and wondering what he was going to do, and then Sly mentioned that he missed his parents, too.

Spider Boy continued to share some things with Sammie and Justin, "We have those moments when we come together and share certain mishaps, those things that are private with each other, so that we can stay strong." Sly also mentions to the children, "Make those boards for your mom and your dad, to honor them for what they taught you. Create those boards for them.

Don't even think about me", he says jokingly, "and put all the pizzazz and color onto those boards and bring them to life for your parents." Sly was aware, that Justin's father was still alive but Justin's father was having complications coping with StarDrome's vibration, just to stay alive. Justin's father's name was Charles, and it was indeed difficult for Justin to watch his father fading.

Sly could sense that Justin was coping fairly well, Justin's dad knew of the dangers associated with the red spheres of energy at night. Every cell soul knew of the dangers in the night, and to be back at their pods when it was dark.

Charles knew of the harmful effects that the sphere could do to his form, as part of his skin was burnt, and the cell souls couldn't recognize him. Charles's right side was damaged, there wasn't anything to repair his burn with; he suffered extremely.

On StarDrome, the cells must house Charles or anyone else that was hurt and dying, in a isolated domicile. So, no one has contact with them, due to radiation. But, as cell souls, we make them as comfortable as possible, until they are ready to expire and decay.

The masters tried to heal his wounds, but it was too severe and Charles knew he was dying and that he would be placed somewhere different, to protect the others. All Justin could do was comfort his father and let him know he's not alone.

Justin does attempt to bring him fresh food daily. As with others; Justin was aware that he had to learn many things from his father and all the wisdom that he could learn and be taught, with Sly's support. With new ideas and ventures on StarDrome, Justin knew they all were in great hands, as the masters prepared beforehand.

Sly felt that the children needed some quiet time on their own, because he believed that this was the time to grieve. But Sly knew he couldn't keep them in that grief for long, because he wanted to strengthen them through their energy. In that moment, Sly thought, 'How could things go so wrong?'

As humans we were once happy; now we are on StarDrome without parents or guardians, as we were told by Master Silver Cloud, that our parents would leave because their bodies couldn't handle the energies of StarDrome.

Sly realized in that moment, he was taking on the burdens of grief, because his thoughts went back to all his loss, as well. Now Sly would need to clean his own energy fields, his own space, so that he could work with the children with clarity.

Master Shade would sense the changes in his energy, when they meet later, to practice shape shifting. Spider Boy recognized that once he took on extra students, he would wake up certain cell memories within himself; that he would recognize he had to heal, he appreciated that.

Sly had to remain focused, so he could distinguish through his energy, what were his memories and what energy belonged to his students.

So, it's all good. Sly quietly gets up and leaves the study room, he reminds Sammie and Justin to finish their boards, for their parents. At that point, Sly then chose to sit outside the door, on the left and proceed to send some positive messages to his parents, and to all the parents of the children, on StarDrome.

Because SpiderBoy understood that his students needed this energy healing, as do the parents. Sly knew in that moment the healing energy was being received, Sly could see them smiling and looking down at him spiritually, through his visions.

SpiderBoy let the parents know telepathically, that he was going to be there on StarDrome teaching and watching over the children. While the masters watched over him and others on StarDrome. Sly also knew within his heart what he felt and agreed to, not just telepathically.

Sly identified that once he made a commitment that he would need to live by that pledge. Spider Boy decided through his intuition to take things to council any concerns or questions that any mentor had; they could take to council.

Then, the council of masters would determine what is best for the students, as they grow and heal. Sly knew he was going to be the best that he could be, each day; as a new day. SpiderBoy believes in giving everyone a fair opportunity, a chance to do things, just like he was given. Spider Boy then comprehends that everyone is learning and growing on StarDrome.

At that moment, Sammie comes running through the door all excited, with her board in her hands. Sammie wants to show Sly the wonderful picture she drew. Suddenly, Sly awakens from his trance and looked at that picture and was amazed by how he could feel the crystal energy, flowing from Sammie's board.

Sly recognizes that Sammie put so much detail into her work, as he gestured to her, he was coming. He then felt the energy of a beautiful amethyst, one of many different crystals Sammie was holding. He knew Sammie was growing fast and he would need to get some other crystals, so that she could start working with the energy.

Sammie went running back into the room as Sly got up and trailed behind her. Just as Sly entered the room, all this wonderful energy embraced him. But, Sly realized all the energy he felt, was flowing from both Justin's and Sammie's boards.

The energy was strong and he thanked both of them for the wonderful work they did. Sly knew in his heart that he was teaching them about energy and how energy maneuver's around things. Then, Sly kind of noticed that Justin wasn't done yet with his creations and walked over to him and looked at his board.

Sly said, "Wow." Justin could hear Sly quite loud and he said, "Oh." and grinned sheepishly. Justin asked Sly if it was possible to keep the boards, Sly already knew that they both wanted to keep the boards and art they made but it had to be kept in the sacred room.

Sly replied, we will make one for your parents and then the other things must be kept. Sly knew in his heart that it was important to keep the things they learnt safe, this way the masters could have a look at what Sly and other mentors were teaching to their students.

It was one of the things the masters treasured, of all mentors. Sly gazes at Justin, saying, "We're going to shrink those things you both made and store them later because everybody has a special place to store things in the sacred warehouse.

Everything needs to be shrunk down to a certain size so that the cell souls can limit the space they use. Then others have use of their sacred space as well, because there is so many of us on StarDrome." Justin felt good about that decision because he knew in his heart that it felt right. Justin trusted what Sly said, because in Sly's eyes the energy spoke 'truth'.

Then everyone took a deep breath and felt good in this day. Everyone knew with all the hard work and creative energy in the day that things were going great. The boards looked and felt awesome, as they resembled portraits, which supported Sly and his new family on StarDrome. SpiderBoy could see many smiles on the faces of the parents before him.

Sly did notice those apparitions appear around him, because the energy felt and looked very good to him. SpiderBoy is learning to discern the positive with the negative forces around him, through his gifts.

He telepathically thanks Sammie and Justin and then proceeds to let them know that he'll see them later, "just before the sun goes down". The energy of excitement filled the room, as they all went on their way smiling.

4

Master Silver Cloud

Wisdom Shared

Sly's up early; He realized while working with Sammie and Justin, he needed to be up before they arrived. Sly already established that he needs to get stronger and disciplined in regards to the things that he needs to teach, if he was going to be a good mentor.

Consequently, Sly finished his morning routine and still had 15 minutes to spare, before the kids got there. Sly sensed after he spoke with Sammie and Justin the day before, that he was being reminded to go to the healing room, today.

The reason was to meet the other mentors that were also teaching students, like him. The masters agreed it was imperative to know of each other on StarDrome. Eleven mentors including Sly knew that they were all meeting today and will come to learn about each other's gifts.

The sacred space where they all intend to gather, will be blessed with special energy, to remind them why they were chosen. Only certain cells were picked from the old world, for this responsibility on StarDrome.

Sly was prepared to meet the old ancient one, the master that was present on old earth while the devastation occurred. Even before Sly's parents even knew, of the Old One, he came and visited in mother's dreams, telling her, she would give birth to a son and he would be special; as many souls were being born.

It was kind of awkward for Sly, knowing that he is an old soul, and that he is going to meet an ancient soul. A soul that's been around for so many journeys, he could probably sit and share many stories, that ancient one.

Sly hears his students coming and it reminds him that he has a few minutes left to finish his tasks. Sly's eager because the paintings that Sammie and Justin drew yesterday on their boards, really opened his eyes to how strong his students were becoming.

This will definitely keep SpiderBoy on his toes and then he giggles to himself. Sly then starts to think to himself, 'the crystal energies', the power Sammie already carries, is very unique, and she doesn't realize it.

Sly is deep in thought, as he sees Sammie coming. She's going to be opening portals and closing doorways, with her crystal energy. Sly stares at Sammie, and realizes that he will need to teach her to honor the things; that the new world carries and shares as minerals.

Sly grasps that he'll be teaching her where to place the crystals, in certain directions to bring healing to the ground on StarDrome. Sly feels over whelmed in the moment, as he is still young, he acknowledges that he must work harder than ever.

StarDrome has a lot to offer and all the cell souls are busy with the earth, water and plants, all life. The Old Teacher will go with others into the energy doorways to work with the grids on StarDrome.

Sly then leaves his trance and looks down and he sees the children standing there, looking up at him. As he was just thinking of all those things, they both smile and say 'hello' to him.

With happiness and excitement Sammie looks into Sly's eyes and silently asks him,' why do you have to go to the healing room today?!' 'Why not tomorrow' Justin said openly; and Sly stares at Sammie and Justin then proceeds to say, "Well, one day you'll both be going there, too.

But right now, I need to meet the other mentors. Justin said abruptly, 'There are others and they are a mentor like you?' Sly replied, we're here on StarDrome to gather and learn about our gifts and our unique responsibilities, that's why I'm going to the healing room today."

They both observed Sly with tender faces and nodded, then Justin replied, "Well, I'm very proud of you, Sly, I mean SpiderBoy', for doing all of those things. Then Justin and Sammie gave Sly a big hug and said out loud together, 'You know you don't need to, but you do', we are proud that you took on this responsibility and we are glad you are our teacher'.

Justin was strong in his delivery, as he pointed out one more thing,' I don't think that I would have wanted it any other way.' Then Justin smiled and said to Sammie, 'let's go, because SpiderBoy has things to do'. Well, I don't mean that, I think, well, you know what I mean."

Then Justin chuckles, looks at Sammie and gives her a hug and Sly looks down at both of them and declares, "Well, I'm very proud of both of you, for your accomplishments yesterday.

For the energy and the colors you both were using on your boards. Forgive me that I was tired; I had a long day myself, as I was training with Master Shade and working with you both.

' Don't mind me when I get that way'. As I'm aware that need to learn how to use my energy and keep it balanced as much as I can.

Plus, I need to learn how to keep it in reserve, so I'm not worn out by the end of the day. So come here and give me a hug because I'm going to go to the healing room now.' Sly just grinned from ear to ear, as he felt proud being a mentor.

I must meet the others shortly, and it goes by very quick.' because as you know we're not in human time anymore'. As I can feel the energy nudging and poking me, as it reminds me that I need to be there.

We all have a certain place that's positioned, in our energy, which we need to match. 'Have fun with the great one', because he'll be teaching you both many new things today, as well.

Sly then smiled and said,' make sure you both stay to the left and follow that pathway', and it will lead you both to the masters place and I'll catch up to both of you later."

"OK," said Sammie and Justin together. "We'll talk to you later. Bye SpiderBoy."

"OK, take care." Sly said, as he followed the winding path to the healing room, he could see all the different butterflies and creatures coming to life around him. They were going in different directions and doing the things they were guided to do.

Every living thing on StarDrome knew and understood what to do through energy, Spider Boy knew everything was connected; he could feel it throughout his body.

Sly was deep in thought thinking; 'we just need to get along and work with each other, as it's one of the rules of this new world. We chose as cell souls, to assist each other and make sure that balance is created on StarDrome.

We are all unique through our gifts, and then Sly bows his head to the right, to honor the memory of all parents. But with gratitude and appreciation for the teachers that are on StarDrome.

Sly then recognizes that he is learning and he is a teacher too. Spider Boy acknowledges and understands that everyone on StarDrome are teachers to each other.

Spider Boy continues his journey down the pathway and he sees the healing room just ahead of him.

Sly gets closer to the room, it actually gets bigger and taller in size. Sly can sense everybody has assembled themselves already; Sly begins to notice that the healing room has become very expansive in energy because of all the energy of the mentors.

To Sly, it feels like everyone present wouldn't fit in this space, but he knows spiritually they will. As things are different on StarDrome because of the cell soul's energy; we'll all learn to adapt to each other's energy and to cell's vast gifts.

SpiderBoy appreciates the guardians at the doorway to the healing room and Sly discerns that the guardians are aware of everyone. From what Sly can see in his visions, there are 11 mentors seated with the old master of the star gate, now twelve including him.

The humbleness in the healing room for the old one is over whelming at first, for Sly. The guardians motion Sly to walk towards his left, and they remind him telepathically to do the full circle.

The full circle is to honor all participants, who sit there in that sacred space. Sly must walk that circle four times

53

before he can find his sitting place. Sly proceeds to his left and then makes his full circle by not interrupting anyone else and that also meant in thoughts.

Sly kept his energy to himself in his aura, within a four foot proximity around him. Everyone present knew telepathically and energetically, that they need to stay within that four feet proximity.

Or else they're getting into someone else's space. Sly continues his walk around the circle four times and he recognizes others that are being seated. Then this reminds Sly to finish and to sit quietly to where he is guided and he automatically comes to a resting place in the Eastern doorway.

Sly sits and prepares himself for the meeting by going into meditation. At that point Sly notices energetically that everyone is sitting quietly and humbly within their energy fields. He witness's everyone starting to float one foot above the floor.

Sly knows intuitively that he's been practicing this discipline every day, and he feels confident and continues to go into trance. This way he continues to raise his energy and then he starts to rise off the floor too.

Sly acknowledges that anyone doing this exercise must have a clear mind and energy. No thoughts from the past or from outside, the master's say,' this exercise takes practice, to be present'.

Sly knows of other cell souls on StarDrome learning to hold their energy as well. Sly gazes around and notice's that some of the mentors' are having difficulty holding their energy.

Some of the mentors are trying to raise their body off the floor and then Sly smiles to himself. As he likes to smile to himself, he realizes that this exercise is a task for him as well. Then Sly reminds himself,' to clear the mind is to clear the thoughts.

Therefore he goes to a special place in his heart, memories of his mother and father, when he was younger. Sly smiles and feels content with those memories; it makes him feel happy as he senses his body elevating.

In his trance, Sly lifts a foot off the ground and as he's looking down. Sly could see the earth energy, it's green. In his visions, it looks like a room full of vines and leaves that hold everyone up in the air.

Everyone is being positioned so uniquely, wonderfully and delicately. Every person is finding their peace place, within their heart through their happy memories. All of the mentors were sitting quietly, here in this sacred space, the mentors don't say a word, and we keep their thoughts very quiet.

Each mentor could tune in and be present and then they remind each other to keep their peaceful energies and quiet their thoughts. The mentors recognize that the master will come into the sacred space, when he knows that everyone is settled and quiet, when the energy is clear.

All of the mentor's breathing, needs to be labored right in the chest, through the heart chakra, as they do their own energy shifting. The Old One will acknowledge immediately, who is concentrating.

Sly senses his own breathing, as he connects and aligns with everyone that's in the room, through sacred breathing. The room is powerful; the energy is good and strong from each mentor. Sly can sense why each mentor in this room was chosen, and he knows they will all grow and become stronger together.

Sly identifies with the flow of energy, within his heart, as they all grow and connect quickly. He realizes to himself, that it doesn't feel like the mentors had a childhood either, as they all grew quicker from one age to the next.

It is through the wisdom in the energy, the mentors grow, and they do not have age or numbers on StarDrome. Sly expresses that thought, as he quietly sits, as cells; we all have memories to keep clear on StarDrome.

Everyone in the room is positioning themselves around the center of the circle, through their meditative thoughts in the same similar way.

Through this expansion of energy, all the mentors radiate. SpiderBoy expresses through his thoughts, that they won't feel the same as when they first came to StarDrome.

Everyone is connected, all of the cells, and they all have their disciplines and knowledge.

SpiderBoy can sense the energy in the room quiet, into this blissful relaxed state as they all know and connect to the master. Master is preparing himself to come into the healing room any time now.

The mentors didn't know from what direction the master was coming, the master's name is Silver Cloud and he chose the name Shade. Shade carries the medicine of 'Silver Cloud' and can pierce through any doorway.

We all choose to honor him, as Master Shade - Silver Cloud and he can change into the element of wind whenever he chooses.

Working with the elements, takes years of practice and commitment. Through this medicine, it helps our crops, water and the very things that sustain each cell soul on StarDrome. In that moment, all the mentors start to align and connect, feeling the master's energy within the sacredness of each breath.

Master Shade then appears in the center of the circle, his energy is all around the mentors, settling in, so gently. Suddenly with strength and purpose Silver Cloud's energy comes flowing from the center of the floor, and it wraps around them as leaves and vines, that hold them up.

Everyone was amazed by what they could feel; they could feel the healing energy start to flow into the base of their spines, as it filled their energy systems (bodies) up.

Master Silver Cloud was aligning to their energy in that moment and it felt so good, the energy frequencies of the mentors were rising. As Master Shade works with them, they all start to notice a red line of energy that comes directly from him, to all of them.

This red energy sits in the base of their spines and aligns back to Shade. Master is very experienced in these energy exercises and he can shape into anything he chooses. Master Shade is very light and dense through his energy and very quiet; his strong telepathic abilities keeps all the mentors on their toes.

The mentors could sense Master Shade gazing around the room quietly, telepathically, watching and listening. His senses are strong; Master Shade distinguishes now that the mentors can connect to all energies through their hearts and souls.

Master Silver Cloud is scanning their systems now and he's reading (seeing) through his visions; their journeys, pathways and memories and he downloads the information within seconds.

Then he puts his books beside him, the books are the catalogues that carry their energy blueprints, as he works with them. Master Shade is busy doing all these things, so quickly, with everyone in the room, it's silent.

(Not a mouse was squeaking, Sly thinks and smiles to himself) Sly starts to notice that the mentors were feeling a little tired because they we're still getting used to running energy. Plus, they are still getting used to working with the energy and Master Silver Cloud.

Master is finished with his scanning and everyone starts to go back down from the position they were hovering in. Until Master Shade can see that everyone touches the ground, safely and quickly.

Through this exercise, when each mentor is seated again, this is how they acknowledge that Master Shade is done. This way they can continue their lessons, and the mentors wait for Master to finish downloading telepathically.

Then he can share these programs with them, and he has a gift for each mentor, at the end of the class. Master has been told by the Old Ones before him, what he needs to do, as he knows that the mentors need to receive more knowledge.

All the mentors will be meeting with Master Shade weekly so that they can improve their gifts and telepathic energies. All mentors were unique and in that moment, Sly reaches back down to the ground and feels light and empty, he's notices that his energy is stronger, faster, and powerful.

Sly can feel the energy and see it coming from his hands and feet. The energy is green and yellow with bits of blue, and he's surprised by his energy.

Sly gazes around the room and he sees that other mentors are admiring their energy as well, sly notices they are all different colors and vibrations. Sly could see in his visions the different vibrations and frequencies of energy, everyone was working with.

Master Silver Cloud shape-shifts back into his form, then stands in the center of the healing room. He then welcomes all of the mentors telepathically, and he lets them know that he'll start his work, from the left side of the circle.

Then Master will share the energy and messages that he was shown; as he downloaded information from their blue prints. All of the mentors take notice, that Master Shade's senses are very strong, and can see future prophecies.

Master Shade has this beautiful silver pillow he sits on and his energy floats above the ground and he asks everyone telepathically if they are ready, and everyone agrees.

He proceeds to share messages and teachings to the mentors on his left, and Master sees Sly sitting there in the circle. Suddenly, Master motions to Sly to come over to his right side and then telepathically proceeds to talk to everyone else.

In that moment, Master Silver Cloud thinks out loud and looks directly at Sly, and this was what Sly heard; "so I see that you are SpiderBoy'. I see that you are red and black in your colors!' You are strong and carry your energy well.' Later you will have three spots on your back as you grow; each spot will represent something new for you.

SpiderBoy, 'You will learn about your spots as you grow and you will notice that you have fine hairs on your legs. Throughout your body these fine hairs will help you to move quickly.

'Your fine hairs will also keep the things off your back, and off your whole body; that will harm you.' Then Master Shade said something that Sly felt in his heart;' later your mother will come in apparition and she will share with you the things you need to know, about your venom."

Then Master Shade smiled; and moved around the circle, sharing messages etc. Sly looked inquisitive and his thoughts went back to his mother right away, and Master had to remind him telepathically to keep his thoughts in the moment.

Master then reminded Sly not to stray away as he was sharing with the group. Master Shade reminded the mentors that they were in that circle to stay present. 'Please connect to what I'm sharing, stay with what you're learning'.

As Master said that, a silver cloud came around the room to quiet the thoughts of everyone in that circle. Everyone started to feel grounded again and SpiderBoy just put his head down and became more humble, and realized that he must learn to listen.

As the other mentors in their circle received that same message, telepathically; we were all grateful in that moment. Silver Cloud said to SpiderBoy, "you will learn. You will also learn how to use your webs and your webs are there to protect you, to keep you safe, also."

Unexpectedly, SpiderBoy had one tear coming from his right eye, as he felt very good with what he had just heard and he sensed it in his heart. Sly then telepathically thanked Master Shade for his wisdom as he sat quietly listening to the other messages that Master Shade had to share.

In the circle, to the left of Sly, sat Mel and he was the oldest boy in the group, he was 19. Sly recognized there wasn't that many mentors that were older than that plus there was a reason.

Sly realized that these other mentors were all different ages and he had to remind himself that it wasn't the age that was important; it was the wisdom. Sly then realized he had to learn to quiet his thoughts again so he could hear what Master Shade was saying.

Mel shape-shifted into 'Gorilla Walks, he was strong, then Master Silver Cloud shared with him,' you are protective; you're also a gatekeeper and a rock keeper. You come from a long generation of buddle carriers, they all have different medicines. Your blood line is mixed with Navaho and Cherokee. Then Mel's dark brown eyes got very big, and he said, "thank you;" great warmth and wisdom came from his eyes when Mel gazed at Master Shade.

"Then Master spoke and said,' your colors are blue and black, "and you must be careful, as you lose your fur every few days. It will take you a few days to grow your fur back, but when you don't have fur, you have no power and can't shape shift," Master Shade said.

"But as soon as your fur grows back, you have your power; you must always remember that'. We will go into the caves and work with the rock people at a later date. The rock people will support you and share with you the history and journeys, of the passages we've been on, throughout time.

It's very good, alleged Master Shade. Gorilla Walks nodded his head, to agree with what Master was sharing and just kept humble. All the mentors felt the energy of gratitude fill the room, everyone was connecting. Master Shade continues sharing his messages, as he looks past Mel, he notices Luna seated on his left; She is called' Swift One and she runs like the speed of light.

Luna is a red haired beauty with deep blue eyes; and she shape shifts easily into a horse. 'Your very fast for 13 yrs.',," said Master Shade. You are from a great blood line of Irish and Mi'kmaq. "You will learn many things about yourself and you will be a carrier for many; because of your speed.

Your mother will also come to visit you in spirit and share with you about your gifts and your silence is your power and your gentleness is your key." Luna was very happy, she felt connected to her energy, as a swift one, and she smiled quietly at both Sly and Mel, and everyone in circle.

Luna felt welcome and safe around all the mentors, and she felt strong energy coming from everyone in the circle. She quietly thanked Master Shade and then Master starting sharing messages with Jamie. We are all aware of how you lost your parents, Jamie. But you come from an important lineage. Do you realize that your lineage fought hard and are great warriors; your parents were both English. The stories are written in the Book of Truth when you're ready to hear them. But I must share with you..."You are a silver fish", said Maser Shade. "You can slide and fit into anything, anywhere and then Jamie's eyes grew restless, and in that minute Master Shade heard her thoughts.

As everything was telepathic and he whispered to Jamie, "Do not fret. You will be ok. You will turn silver with blue flecks, on your back. Master Shade had caution in his eyes." Master sensed Jamie was scared, and then he reassured her to quiet her thoughts because Jamie was only four.

Master Shade quietly stated to Jamie, when you hold your gaze on someone, you'll freeze them and turn things into ice. Jamie, you will learn how to work with this later in life, when you are older in a few years.

The mentors noticed Jamie had tears coming from her eyes, as she said, she loved the color silver. Through her vision, she could see her silver hands and feet and she felt proud to be a silver fish. Within that second, she closed her eyes with Master Shade and with the other mentors. Everyone connected telepathically with her energy, as a silver fish; so she wouldn't be afraid.

Everyone then knew that this was Jamie's power, and then she smiled and cried. Jamie was grateful to everyone in the room, and she kept that in her thoughts. Then Master Silver Cloud continued around the circle, to Jamie's left; and saw Star.

Star was a bit older than Jamie, by two years. She was six, and Master Shade gently telepathically said to Star, "you already know who you are, as you've seen this in your visions." Star smiled and said 'yes'.

"You are Star Fish," said Master Silver Cloud; and then Star smiled. "You are Star Fish and you can stick to the faces of any enemy, and you have lethal toxins; that knock out any prey for ten minutes, Master said with discernment" But, you will work with your energy further, as you grow; similar to Jamie'.

Master shared such deep messages with Star, as she smiled the biggest smile. Everyone could see her grin; from ear to ear. Suddenly, Jamie said to Master Shade 'can I have permission to speak', but Master Shade knew that Jamie was asking permission, to remind the other mentors about respect.

Master understood everything was being said in a good way, and he let her proceed. Then Star said, "I see my colors, as orangey yellow, and I'm very shiny in the light.

Plus, I turn dark blue in cold temperature and can freeze.

Jamie then smiled the biggest smile and Master Shade said "yes."

Sly realized everyone felt happy for her and smiled as well, and Master Shade asked once again. 'Star, "you must be careful in the cold, as you know; there is a place on StarDrome... Then Master stopped his thoughts and pulled his energy back, then continued to say to Star; if you hold your prey for more than ten minutes, they go blind, if you're angry.

Jamie knew that she had the energy of anger to work through, to heal; frustration is where you start to learn, to change your behavior. 'So, always remind yourself to work through your frustrations and as Master Shade finished sharing with Star, she knew what he meant and quietly looked down.

Jamie knew within her heart that she needed to work through those things, as she felt frustrated all the time. Jamie kept repeating to herself,' don't get mad;' don't get frustrated'...she reflected on her night terrors of her family being tortured...this was on Old Earth. She knew in that moment, she had to find them one day when she was older. Jamie remembered her mother the best because she taught her about cleansing ceremonies and she once had her own eagle feather. Jamie believes in her heart she is Cree, then she looked up at Master Shade and shook her thoughts off and Master then said to everyone, "Take a deep breath."

Then he moved on to George, "George you are ten, much older than your years, and sometimes you don't want to be here." George felt embarrassed to answer Master Shade and Master Shade said, "It's ok, we all grow and learn through many teachings and lessons."

Master then whispered to George, "Who are you, George? What do you see? As, you have had visions before in your dreams. George looked down, and then looked around, and he telepathically said quietly to Master;

Just as George was going to share, Master Shade had to remind George to speak up. "Make sure that your thoughts are clear." Then, George cleared his mind through his breathing and replied, "I am Tiger Running"

"Hmmm", said Master Shade. "You are correct. You are the color brown with one black stripe, down your back." George knew that was true, he could feel all the energy run up his back. Then and there Master Shade said to George, "You can run, leap and capture any prey within seconds. You will notice on the left side of your face, your eye tooth releases toxins into the blood streams of any enemy.

The toxins then drive your prey crazy, and it leads to their sudden death." Master Silver Cloud suggested to George, 'you can use this gift in a couple of years, as you get stronger; it is your choice.

This lesson will also teach you to eat only on your right side, or you will re – lease the toxins into your own blood stream. Then with a stern voice, Master said out loud,' you cannot eat on your left side." Only Mazie can assist you with the medicine from a unique flower; and it only grows in the Badlands and is protected by the elves…

George looked confused and said to Master Silver Cloud, telepathically, "Yes. I'm aware of that, or else my food doesn't taste great." And he smiles…and deeply thinks about what Master Shade had shared and smiled at Mazie.

The other mentors tried not to chuckle with George, and Master Shade had to remind everyone "quiet" and George was pleased with what he heard, and then Master Shade moved on to Mazie.

Master Silver Cloud noticed Mazie was shy, self-conscious, and she was only sixteen. To Master, it felt like Mazie still needed her mother, but Mazie knew that she had to leave her mother's side because she was weakening, and wouldn't be on StarDrome long.

Master Shade knew Mazie was sad, so he helped Mazie clear her mind, through her thoughts so she couldn't blame herself, for her mothers' choices. Master then asked Mazie quietly about her mother... and before Master Shade could get anything out, Mazie quickly whispered, "I am Flower Power." My mother called me flower for short...because I love flowers. She grew a lot of flowers in different planter pots and caressed them every day, she was from Tokyo. My mother wanted to attend the Senso-ji in Asakusa, but they wouldn't accept her because she was too young. She always whispered in my ear as I was growing,' my little Flower of Peace...

Mazie then smiled and hugged Master Shade. The room grew very quiet, as the mentors knew not to hug Master Shade, because Master has thin skin and he must be careful.

Mazie felt strong when she shared telepathically with Master Shade.

In that moment Mazie smiled, and Master said, "Yes, Mazie, you are the Flower of Peace. You can camouflage yourself to match all terrains and you can also release deadly pollen, to anyone trying to hurt you." Master Shade then mentioned to Mazie, 'you will learn more about this gift, later'.

Mazie was surprised and shared with enthusiasm, "I release deadly pollen?" All the mentors looked at her and said telepathically,' you are important Mazie'; "Yes," said Master Shade. ""And I see that you love purple."

Mazie smiled and agreed with Master Shade, "I do love purple,"" and then Master reminded Mazie: "Purple puts others to sleep with the pollen of the flowers.

"The flowers don't work without the purple energy. Mazie looked down and then looked up at Master Shade, and said, "What?" "Yes, purple puts others to sleep, but the flowers pollen doesn't work without it. If you wear the color purple, you can put someone to sleep for a few minutes.

Mazie looked around and the others chuckled, and then Master said, "Quiet" and Mazie replied, "you're right." For a moment I thought the mentors were just ignoring me, I thought they were just bored and then everyone in the room chuckled and said,' we pretended to be asleep.

Master Shade then let out a little grin,' Now you know,' and Mazie said quietly, "Oh. I guess I need to work on that one. But I still love purple." Next, Master Shade moved onto Alex, and whispered, "Alex. You're 11."

Alex nodded at Master Shade and felt good about being eleven and fair-haired with some freckles; master noticed he was grumpy in the morning, as Alex isn't a morning person. Alex knew and understood what master was saying, because he did believe he resembled his father that way. Alex remembers his father always being grumpy with him and his mom Louisa. Alex then proceeded to share with the group that his mother came from Mexico and that his dad fell in love with her right away…then he took her to the U.S.A…

Master Shade reminded Alex that mornings were very important, and mentioned to him that he would adjust, and his shape-shifting name is Jelly Stinks." Then Alex looked at Master Shade and rolled up his nose, and said, "What? My name is Jelly Stinks?"

Then everyone tried to be quiet, not sending any telepathic thoughts Alex's way, knowing that jelly does stink. Master Silver Cloud said, "Yes, jellies stink. You're lime green and your color emits a dangerous gas."

Alex's blue eyes looked up at Master and he smiled the biggest smile, and Alex knew that it was 'OK to be Jelly Stinks'. Master Shade then proceeded to say,' that dangerous gas, causes choking and instant death', and then Alex grinned, "ooh, really?" Then Alex thought,' how do I protect others from this gas?'

"Yes", said Master Shade. "You need to be very cautious, something you will be learning. But you must stay in the water during the day." Alex frowned and he said to Master Shade, "why?"

"Well," said Master Shade, "you can come out at night, but only as a shape-shifter. As Jelly Stinks, you must stay in the water all day, or you will dry up and your powers will fade." Today is an exception!

At that point, Alex said, "OK." It gave him some serious food for thought. Alex was thinking, I hate water,'

"Hmm," said Master Shade. "Wonderful, gifted ones here, in this sacred space. Let's move on to Lena."

Beautiful, dark haired Lena, beautiful smile, a bit quiet, little reserved, said Master Shade, when you are shape-shifting into Space Envy you must control your temper. Lena was OK with that because she understood it because of her parents, and what they taught her. As they are both gone now and are both from an Italian lineage...Lena knew how much they adored her, as she was their only child...

Lena you will be turning 13 any day now; and you have learned many things about being reptilian. Master Silver Cloud said to her telepathically, "You are a reptilian, and have spikes running all the way down your spine, can you feel them?"

Lena nodded and she telepathically said yes, I have felt them since I was three. I didn't question it", she alleged, "Because I knew that they were part of me." "Hmm," said Master Silver Cloud, "Very well, we will move on.

" He pronounces to Lena, "You also have webbed feet and hands; and you must stay in the water, for a certain amount of time. This way your skin doesn't dry and crack because you will notice it, the cracks will produce massive bleeding, throughout your body.

Then Master added,' if you are in the water too long, you will wrinkle and bloat; so you must find a balance between both." Lena already knew the lessons involved because she felt both and she didn't feel good with being wrinkly or cracked. Because, Lena knew her skin would feel too tight and she wasn't able to use her magic too well.

Lena was aware, if she dried, it felt like she was choking, so she agreed with Master Shade, to keep the balance between water and land. "I agree with that, she said politely,' Thank you."

Master then looked at Lena and said, "Another thing,' you also hypnotize others; through your eyes." Within that moment, she gazed at Master Shade and then looked around the room quickly.

Trying to have contact through her eyes', and then Master Shade said,' Lena, "Not yet. But, you will also learn to rein your 'gifts', I won't share with you now, but I will later." When you learn to hypnotize, you will notice that it will last for a few hours.

Lena felt very good with what she had heard, from Master Shade. All the mentors knew of their 'gifts' and of everyone in the room, they all felt good and comfortable with each other. Master still had to share messages with two more mentors.

"Hmm," said Master Shade. "A dozen mentors, we are missing some. We have other mentors from other blocks on StarDrome; they are preoccupied with other exercises and you will meet them at a later date.

I love all of your energy, you are all very powerful and the things that you learn will strengthen your skills. Well, let's move on to Max." "Ah, Max," whispered Master Shade as he shakes his head.

Max tries not to look at Master Shade, but he looks up at him because he needs to get eye contact, because this is how Max learns to listen.

'Max you're learning to be a good listener because lately you haven't been listening and you have gotten into trouble and mischief. You have been working hard in the fields and gardens and I don't need to say more, explained Master Shade; as he continues to share his wisdom with him.

'You shape-shift into Lion Heart; Yes, Lion Heart and through this gift you will find your courage and strength. You shift into a big light brown feline and you are working with honoring your female side. But you must not mate as a female because you were born male.

Sometimes as masters, we will see some mentors choose to stay female as this helps them heal. Then Max replied and said,' why Master Shade?'

Then Max starting purring right after that, everyone was trying not to chuckle, but it was something that Max did all the time, especially if he was tired and he telepathically asked Master Shade, "could I share something with you and the class?"

"Sure," said Master Silver Cloud. "Go ahead." So, Max said, "I have whiskers and I can grow them very fast.' I noticed them when I was small and I can use my whiskers as darts'. Well, how do I know that!

"Is it OK if I share this, Master Shade?" Master Shade nodded. "Yes." It shows me you have been paying attention to what happens as you grow and shape shift. "Well I accidentally threw one dart on my right foot and it hurt.' I still have a tender spot there and it is purple and black and it won't go away."

"Well," said Master Shade, "I will help you with that." Then Master Shade walked over to Max, the Lion Heart, and he put his index finger from his right hand down on his foot in that same tender place and presto! Master mentioned to Max, you can learn a lot about your medicines from your Swedish ancestors...

Within that second the bruises and tenderness were gone. Max looked at Master Shade and smiled. Master observed the mentors around the room and quietly went back to his position, and then finished sharing with Max.

"I'll explain more about that later," said Master Shade. "Now, you don't want to get wet. Or it changes your fur to a deep, deep purple." As soon as Flower Power heard that, well, you know what Mazie would have thought and she tried to pull her thoughts back to herself before others picked them up.

Then Master Shade said to Max, "and if you stay wet for a long period of time, the color will stay with you until it subsides, but you also don't have your powers when you're purple." Max felt dumbfounded, and he telepathically asked Master Shade, "Why?"

"Well, it's only temporary" said Master Shade, "until the purple subsides, so you just need to practice to stay out of the water." At that moment Lion Heart telepathically said,

"OK, I guess." and Max was listening to all Master shared; as no one needed to tell him to listen.

Suddenly, Master Shade reminded everybody to take a deep breath and he continued around the circle to share his wisdom with Clayton. "Oh yes," said Master Shade and then everybody took a deep breath and Master Shade said, "So you are Clayton, and you are the second oldest one in the group.

You are 17, and you've been busy learning for many years, as we know. We have learnt many things and you're the leader of this group and if you take ill or pass away then Spider Boy takes over.

SpiderBoy was shocked and then Clayton felt confused and asked Master; 'Why not Mel? He's 19 years old and strong?' Clayton was OK to receive these telepathic messages from Master Silver Cloud because the more everyone understood the better.

So Clayton waited for Master's reply; as he was already aware of the answer. Master Shade said 'I will share that later as everyone knows that Mel is a gate keeper and has other responsibilities on StarDrome. Then Master Shade proceeded to share Clayton's name and how he shape shifts into a winged one.

"You are Raven..." your lineage comes from the coastal islands from an old time... and as soon as Master Shade said those words telepathically to Clayton, everyone in the circle could see Clayton shift into Raven's Face. As soon as he shifted into Raven's Face, everyone could see the color in Clayton's feathers.

They were black like shiny coal as Master shared with Clayton that his feathers were made of steel, and everybody could feel Ravens energy in the room. The mentors felt instinctively that Raven's Face could protect himself anytime, anywhere and he could protect anyone with those wings, but only in certain locations on StarDrome.

Raven's wings were huge and Master Shade didn't really need to say anything more, as Clayton was saying it all telepathically, everyone in the room was energetically connecting to the experience.

Master Silver Cloud then said to Clayton, (to Raven's Face), "Your gaze stops anyone in their tracks; but only for a few seconds, just long enough to change the flow of something negative into positive.' "You have the gift of changing outcomes' but only while your present in the same locality".

At that point Master Shade looked around the circle and felt proud of all the mentors and smiled quietly at everyone. Then he finished sharing with Clayton,' "But you can hold your gaze for a duration of time, for 10 minutes or so, it will also tire you quickly if you try to force the gaze longer.

Then Raven's Face stared at Master and nodded and Master calmly said,' you will automatically and intuitively know in ten minutes;' or your power will weaken and you would need to rejuvenate.

Then everyone noticed how Master Shade's expression grew strong and discerning as he added telepathically. 'There's only a certain tree that you can rejuvenate your system with, and we only have one of those trees on StarDrome, and that tree only grows once'.

'The tree's name is 'Sage' and she will know when you need her, so you must refine your power. Sage can only drink from the one water that SpiderBoy prepares for her and she can only be watered twice in one year; 'or she will die'.

'Sage is only connected to you and SpiderBoy; she will not listen to any other mentor'. Master Shade then glanced at SpiderBoy and Raven's Face, and nodded. Master then added,' the tree already knows of you;' and you will learn of the tree.

'You will already know how to find each other." replied, Master Shade. Clayton and SpiderBoy telepathically said, 'thank you' to Master Silver Cloud, and they both understood exactly what Master had just said.

The other mentors in the group were quite surprised by that information and looked around at each other, realizing that everyone carried a lot of responsibility, as mentors to the younger cells.

Clayton took the information rather well and then all of a sudden Master Shade shouted to everyone, "now shape-shift.' I want to see how you work with your energy together and I choose to see how powerful you are through your visions and senses.

Then Master Shade lifted his energy up through his body, and floated to the ceiling; watching everyone smiling. As all his mentors stretched, expanded and worked with their energy, then the healing room expanded in energy too; so it could house all the shape shifters, in size and shape.

Because, there were so many things going on in front of Master, he decided to block the energy from the outside to keep it private. So with Master, the mentors' practiced for the rest of the day. Master Shade was glad that all the mentors were learning and growing quickly, it was important for them and StarDrome.

5

Crystal Girl and Panther Struts

Two Cells

It's the next day and SpiderBoy is worn, the energy work with Master Shade was pretty intense. Sly realizes with more practice, it will get easier. He knows and understands within his soul, that it's important to be disciplined.

Equally, all the other mentors are aware that these teachings are useful and helpful, not just for themselves but it will bring them the resources needed to teach the children.

As Sly lays there in his bed, his thoughts go back to his mother and father. Sly then wishes in that moment that they were there and desires that the old world wasn't gone; the old world he remembers.

SpiderBoy shakes his head, so he can get rid of those thoughts. Sly realizes that he is living proof and legacy of the things that his parents taught him and being an old soul; he has responsibilities.

Sly appreciates how he feels within himself, as he accepted a lot of responsibility. As he looks into his heart and distinguishes that he would have been lost somewhere in the old world, like others that weren't ready to leave.

As he lay there Sly recognizes how fortunate he is to sit with the other mentors; because they all have sacred tools and gifts to bring to StarDrome. To observe the viewing screen and to read the Akashic records, to work with the crystals, to do the energy work and heal.

Each mentor held gifts and will continue to grow and nurture the water, StarDrome's gardens and land. Sly apprehends within that moment there's lots to be grateful for, ('even thinking that, made Sly tired') He yawns and stretches, then sees that the sun is up and realizes he's got to get ready for Sammie and Justin.

Then Sly jumps up and does his morning routine which includes stretching and yoga. He then aligns his energy through his chakras and does deep breathing. Through his breathing, Sly honors the spirit of his vessel and new skin.

He knows his new skin will protect him on StarDrome. Through his thoughts, Sly starts to realize everyone is protected and he connects his energy to the sun, for strength and purity; there's so much essence in that energy. As Sly is moving and stretching he realizes that everything is deeply connected, every little piece of energy, no matter what it is.

Through his thoughts Sly can hear and connect to who he wants on StarDrome. That flow of energy moves within everything, as below, as above the ground, and everything has a rhythm of frequency and energy source.

Then Sly takes another deep breath and realizes he is connected to the heart and core of StarDrome, the center of all things. SpiderBoy acknowledges that everyone is growing rapidly on StarDrome, and how the dome protects everyone in this new world.

In that moment Sly had to stop his thoughts and come back to his center, so he stretches and brings his arms back to his heart. Then he gives thanks for the new day, the new approach, to all the ones that inhabit StarDrome and to all the parents lost.

Sly then sends messages of healing and gratitude to Master Shade and all the other masters, teachers that are on StarDrome. Then he stands up erect and then stretches again feeling similar to the height of a tree. In that moment, Sly thought, if he was a tree, his branches would reach out to the universe and keep going; until there's no end.

Then he smiled this perfect little grin, knowing inside that there are many possibilities because energy is in everything. Then the knock at his door reminded Sly, it's the kids and he walks over to the door, opens it quietly and peeks at them.

"Hello, what can I do for you?" Sly said, candidly.

Sammie and Justin were standing there with their books, papers and their new vision boards. "We came to draw," they both said together, laughing.

SpiderBoy noticed both kids were feeling light and new. Sly thinks that he should open the door or else the kids would think he's busy with something else. Sly kindly say's to both of them, "Well. We won't be doing a lot of drawing today'.

Then the children casually walk right in, past Sly ignoring him. Then Sly continues to share with the kids, 'Sammie we're going to work with your crystals today and Justin, we're also going to work with your panther. The kids both smiled at Sly as he spoke with them; it is important for both of you to align with your magic.

"Make yourself comfortable and grab a pillow to sit on…' find a place with as much space as possible, thanks!' Sly could then see that Sammie was excited to work with her crystals again, 'I see that you have three or four different crystals," Sly states.

Sammie is all excited and she takes her crystals out of her pocket and then she proceeds to say to Sly and Justin, "These are my little friends and I know that they help me every day and every night." Both Justin and Sly felt the energy as Sammie shared what she said; as she held them in her little hands.

She then utters to them, "and do you really want to know something else?" Justin got excited and he looks at Sammie and says, "What? "Tell us, please.

"Well," said Sammie, "I even put my crystals under my pillow." Justin looks at her with wide eyes and says to her, "Under your pillow?

Why under your pillow?" Justin utters. Suddenly, Sly whispers, "quiet' we need to get situated here, we have things to do. This is going to be a long day again. But, the day moves very quickly as you both know, so find yourself your favorite little place to sit and get positioned."

Sly continued to do the same and then Sammie sits on a beautiful, purple, bluefish pillow. This pillow is for her crystals and Sammie realizes within herself that her crystals need to have a real comfortable place to sit. 'Yes they do', she says to herself, smiling.

As Sammie's getting her crystals ready, Justin's on the left side of the room taking up big space. He's already sensing telepathically that when he shifts he will need all the space he can get. Justin is quietly thinking to himself, and he's looking at Sammie and Sly and said to both of them, "OK, if I bring my panther out, where is SpiderBoy going to be?"

Justin thought to himself saying, I'll just leave that alone; Sly can figure that out. Sly was smiling and slightly shook his head at Justin and replied, "quiet, it's ok, we'll figure it all out'. Everything always works out, just get ready' and as you're getting ready on your pillow, station yourself.

'Make sure your feet are on the ground nice and flat, then bring the palms of your hands together and take a nice deep breath and feel the energy in your body.' Practice connecting your energy with the universe way up high in the sky, through the stars and then just pull all the energy down.'

You will notice sparkly silvery blue energy, bring it down through your head, and feel it through your entire body and remember to breathe'; nice and deep said Sly firmly. 'Uh huh' said Justin and he recognized what energy felt like, in that moment.' What does that feel like?' asked Sly, 'How does the energy feel through your skin, in your tissues, right into your skeleton?'

Is it relaxing; is the energy moving out and what are the colors? 'And just keep breathing in and out, let the energy flow down your arms, feet and just relax into it, "said SpiderBoy calmly."

SpiderBoy could feel and see Sammie getting tingles all over and he notices her trying not to giggle; and in that moment Sammie glances over to the other side of the room and sees Justin and his panther, on his left side.

The panther was introducing his energy to Justin. "Sly suggests to Sammie and Justin, to feel and connect to their vision; through their eye's. "Breathe, please remember to breathe. Now, feel the energy at the bottom of your toes and your feet;' and wiggle them around.

Sly asks both students if they can feel the grounding energy through their feet and chakras. Then Sly mentions that there is a chakra in the center of their feet. 'Now feel the energy go down your legs, through your feet, into the earth and look at the energy as leaves. Beautiful golden copper leaves, very light, iridescent, and make sure, you breathe.'

Sly reassured them. SpiderBoy felt good in that moment, as he could see his pupils were doing an amazing job. Then he asked the children if they noticed how much energy they were running, through their back and tailbone, then into their hips." The children looked relaxed, from what Sly noticed.

He motions to Justin to breathe. "Just work with this energy, Justin and then the panther will know what he needs to do; for himself as he connects to your energy. 'Sammie said Sly, 'you'll notice as you're working with your energy and crystals, you are waking them up energetically.

You'll hear them, so tune in and see what you can perceive and breathe nice and deep, because I can hear your crystals' giggle and laugh," declares Sly.

"What can you hear? Just recognize it. Keep those messages to yourself for now and you'll notice the room will start to slowly spin; as all the energy opens up around us."

Then Sly thinks to himself,' I love crystals' and grins. Then all of a sudden the room was full with light and circles of energy, moving around them. Justin observed the energy around the room and telepathically said, 'Wow,' look at all these beautiful blue and silver energy balls."

As Justin watched the energy dance around him and Sammie, Sly had to remind them again, "make sure you're breathing, because it is a very big piece of what you're doing' Thanks.

It will help you stay present and grounded; it will benefit your energy through your bodies; to stay here."

Justin telepathically asks Sly, "What does that mean, stay here?" "Well, it just means that your spirit, that wonderful beautiful energy that you are, will stay present in your body.

You need to feel your spirit sitting in your body, in the room. 'Yes, feel yourself sitting here, and you'll recognize every little inch of yourself, from your toes, fingers, and shoulders, to your head."

Sly smiled at both of them; while hearing Sammie giggle, again. Sammie telepathically said to Sly, "I can't help it; I can't help giggling because I've all these tickly, fuzzy energies running up my back and arms; and my shoulders and head."

Justin smiled and he telepathically said to Sammie, "I have them too. I just didn't want to say anything."

"Hush, hush," said Sly. "I have them too. We all have them; the energy is symbolic from our relative's, saying they are happy.

All our guides, angels and helpers, are supporting us on StarDrome, through your crystals and shape shifting. We are so blessed, said Sly. We'll talk with them later, they'll support and guide us, but right now you've got to focus on your gifts. Ok?

'So, breathe nice and deep again." Sly mentioned, as he looked more focused; and asks Sammie what she feels, and senses, from her crystals.

"Two years have passed," he said to both of them. "And you're growing very, very, fast, and it's important to understand and connect to these energies because time is moving very quickly.

Within that moment Sly mentions to both of them,' and always relate to your tools with the best intentions and always use your intuition'. Work with your telepathic, telekinesis energies and always honor them; now take a deep breath." Then, Sly does too!

Sly gazes up at Sammie and nods at her to continue, and then Sammie picks up one of her crystals and put's it into her hand. She notice's that it is one of her favorite crystals; it's a beautiful amethyst.

"This is my favorite one she says." And it's hot, there's lots of heat coming from it, it feels very good. Then Sammie sees all the beautiful rays of energy coming from her favorite crystal.

In that moment both Justin and Sly could hear her thoughts very clearly, which is very good and Sammie indicates that her crystal brings healing to the heart.

"I remember this crystal helping me when I was smaller," Sammie utters.

"It was one that I received from my mom." And then she had a tear in her eye, and then she brings the crystal very close to her heart. Just at that time, Justin was trying to keep his thoughts clear too, so he won't think about his parents, and then he continued trying to keep his focus.

Sly takes notice and says, "Now take a deep breath, Sammie. Justin can you do the same, thanks! 'And pull your energy in and breathe again." One breath after each other; then Sly says to Sammie, "Very good. You'll learn about those crystals.

That crystal you're holding will also open a door for you." Then, Sammie just looked at Sly and said, "Ok." Her eyes were dancing, and the energy just felt really good.

Within that moment, he just looks at Sammie and shares, "OK, just put that crystal down on your right side, the one you are holding tightly.

Then notice how the energy from the crystal helps you feel calm. Sly then smiles and reassures Justin to breathe and send loving intentions to his parents too! Then and there Sly loudly says,' and don't forget yourself."

Now you can sense the energy in the room shift, and breathe again. Then Sammie picked up another crystal, this one was smaller. Sly was watching how Sammie was picking the crystal up; and how she was delicately holding it.

Sammie was maneuvering it around, and then Sly looks over at Justin and watches him close his eyes, and noticed he was focusing on all of the things that are being said. Panther is playing quietly and Sly was happy.

"Now, take a deep breath." Sly casually states; And then Sammie looks at this crystal she was holding and says, "This one is a pink fluorite."

Then she smiles at it; "Mm," says Sly. "And what does pink fluorite do for you?"

"Well, this one sometimes makes me cry. I hold it just for a little bit of time and if I hold it too long, I notice I get weepy, said Sammie; Sometimes I can't stop my tears."

SpiderBoy nods and then looks over at Justin, and says to Justin with a thin, long voice, "Justin, did you connect to that energy that Sammie was just sharing, on the pink fluorite?

"I did," said Justin. "As I was tuning into its energy, the fluorite was healing my feet. My feet were tired the other day and I could feel the energy working on my toes. Then Justin smiles and continued sharing;' my feet feel great."

SpiderBoy noticed how much Justin was smiling, and Sly said well. "That's good you're connecting. Great."

Within that moment Sammie put the other crystal down and she picked the third one up, and it was agate. Sammie really didn't know what to say about the agate because she was just learning about agate.

Sly declares, "Its ok. You can hold that agate and work with its energy by holding it in the palms of your hands, it's like if it was putty. 'Sly grins and shares;' Let the energy of the agate move and connect with your energy. Listen to it, what is it saying?

Are you sensing anything from the crystal? Sly asked, and let it be part of your energy as you hold it in your hands. Because what you're doing – then Sly reminds both kids to 'take a deep breath'; you will recognize the energy of this agate introduce itself, to your energy; and this is how you're becoming friends.

Sly smiles again and adds,' this is how your energy is connecting to the energy of the crystal. The agate now knows you're there for it, as it is there for you.

"Remember, we are a part of everything, on StarDrome, So just work with that right now.

Then we can check in after, to see what the energy teaches you." SpiderBoy feels good with everything he is teaching and relaxes. Then he glances at both of them and says telepathically, "take a deep breath, please;" your breathing is important for grounding your energy because your both doing so much.

Sly searches his thoughts for a second and wonders if he is being too hard…then he smiles and say's to himself;' no', they are both fine. Then he gives his head a shake, so he can stay focused.

Sly then chooses to walk over to Justin and positions himself across from him and he looks at Panther Struts and says, "Take a deep breath." A real deep breath,' make sure you feel your breath in your solar plexus.

Then SpiderBoy shows him an example, of breathing; Justin smiles and nods. In that moment Justin takes a deep breath and feels it deep in his gut, and hears Sly saying to him, "put your feet flat on the ground, Justin."

Justin listens to SpiderBoy and uncrosses his legs, puts his feet down and sits up, and then he sees that Sly is working with the energy in his feet and toes. Justin then senses the energy Sly is using and connects, as well.

Sly then mentions to Justin to grab his hands, palm to palm, and shares with Justin, "I want you to run (connect) your energy with mine. So feel the energy in your left palm with the palm of your right hand, and breathe nice and deep.

Notice what you see, hear and sense, then SpiderBoy asks

Justin, 'do you see some beautiful purple and blue colors? Then Sly suggests,' take a closer look and see if you can see the little specks of white in the healing energy. As a reminder, Sly then mentions to the kids again, just breathe and connect to the energy, your both opening up.

As you notice the energy increasing in size, just breathe through the exercise, thanks! And as you're doing that," he then says to Justin, "you must work with the energy as you shape shift;' relax into the flow of the shift. Do what the energy asks of you. Let the energy align, connect and move through your body."

Just as SpiderBoy finished saying what he did, he could see Justin changing into Panther Struts, right in the center of his form, (body), and then Panther is breathing heavily and aligns with Justin's energy.

Sly could see and feel the energy, too, and then Sly starts to shape-shift into SpiderBoy. Suddenly, Sammie looks up at Sly and Justin and is amazed by what she sees; and then she laughs.

"OH, I love this, it feels so wonderful, and please make sure you're breathing," Sly said peacefully. Then he glances at the beautiful red and black colors, on his tough shell. SpiderBoy noticed he is stronger, he could feel the energy on his back and his two main legs.

SpiderBoy acknowledges his senses are keener and those three spots he has, are becoming tougher. Sly knows one of his spots re leases web; but it is really sticky and has a faint smell. Until, SpiderBoy learns to work with it more, the web will strengthen and the smell will fade.

SpiderBoy likes where his web spot is located, on his leg in the front, it's perfect for shooting webs. SpiderBoy knows his right leg is stronger, than the left; because in the Book of Truth it is written…

When Sly was born, he was delivered so rapidly, his mother Charmaine pushed too hastily. Then Sly's leg got caught and twisted in the birth canal; SpiderBoy knows everything is written in the Book of Truth and it can't be seen by others.

Sly knows now, it will always be the same and he'll love and feel good; especially when he connects to his silvery threads of his web, he spins. Then SpiderBoy grinned and took a deep breath, as well.

Sly telepathically connects to Justin, and asks him how his alignment is with panther; "And reminds Justin to breathe, to feel his ears, head and neck." Sly could sense the energy that Justin feels and it's good, strong and so connected.

"Yes, Sly cries and he notices that Justin loves being Panther Struts. Justin takes a deep breath in that moment and connects to his paws. Then Sly says to Justin, "how does that sensation feel when you're connecting to your paws?"

"It feels good, and peculiar. Then Panther Struts replies,' I'm very connected." "Good," says Sly. "Keep going. Breathe nice and deep." SpiderBoy then jumps over to Sammie, and looks down at her, from the ceiling.

Sly loves being a Spider and he realizes that Sammie didn't see him; and he chose to watch her play and connect with her crystals. SpiderBoy could observe everything from the ceiling and he glances at Sammie laying there on her pillow, and she's got one crystal on her forehead.

Wow! Sly said with amazement, to himself and he continued watching her; SpiderBoy decides to come down from the ceiling with his web and notices another crystal; Sammie placed on the center of her third eye.

Sly was amazed by what he was witnessing, as he didn't teach Sammie this, and he comes in even for a closer look. SpiderBoy then notices another crystal Sammie placed on her fifth chakra, (right on her throat). SpiderBoy realized he had two amazing students and this was going to be fun, as he detected the pink tourmaline, sitting on her fourth chakra.

Then tears came to his eyes, Sly knew he was tuned into her emotions because he could see the energy stemming from her heart. Sly can sense Sammie's breathing and felt her relaxing into the energy. In that moment, SpiderBoy wished Master Shade was here to see this, he would be proud.

Sly is very impressed with Sammie and sent her messages of healing, and she smiles at him and continues what she's doing. Suddenly, SpiderBoy drops to the floor with a wallop, and realizes he stayed up on the ceiling to long.

Sly has to get stronger, then his webs can hold him longer; then Sly knew his webs couldn't hold any more weight. SpiderBoy then walks over to the other side of the room and telepathically connects with Justin. SpiderBoy perceives that Justin is shape shifting halfway as Panther, and decides to assist Justin with moving his energy down his spine, legs, and tail.

SpiderBoy had to jump out of the way, suddenly because Panther Struts was huge. Spider Boy immediately feels and connects to the warmth of the energy, as Justin notices the expansion too.

Panther Struts has the strength, power and even the growl; it could be heard from miles away. Well, to Justin it was a growl that he liked and could live with. Sly smiles and he treads over to the left side of the room and he looks down into the energy of Panther Struts; and says to Justin,

"When I count to three, I want you to get up and run."

And Justin telepathically says ok. "One" and Sly counts slowly and motions to Justin to get ready, and then he says, "Two." Then Panther stretches, and arches his back, aligning his energy. At that point sly cries, "Three," and then panther pounces and lands on his front paws, running towards SpiderBoy.

SpiderBoy can see how excited Justin is, when he heard him say loudly; "This is awesome, this is really awesome," says Panther Struts. "I feel brand new. Look at my little whiskers, well they're growing, and look at my new feet." Justin is so happy leaping up and down and he's working hard not to get into Sammie's energy (space); or in her way as she's working with the crystals.

He's all excited and runs around SpiderBoy, within that second, SpiderBoy starts jumping and running after panther and they're both chasing each other around the room. Then SpiderBoy comes back down from the ceiling, before his web gives out; and shape-shifts back into his body, as Sly. Then he looks at Panther Struts and says "Wow, you've done well.

Look at you, you're going to be a big cat, I can see that."

"Now," says Sly, "take a deep breath." Justin takes a deep breath. Now, 'feel that breath in your chest, shoulders, arms and back, Sly shared;' now feel that energy through your feet and then breathe nice and deep again.

Panther Struts senses his energy and acknowledges it, he likes what he feels. Panther can connect to the energy throughout his new form, and then Sly smiles and says to him, 'Yes, you have found your way.' Now you've found your connection, your heart-piece';

Now take a deep breath, count to three telepathically and then shape-shift back into you, as Justin." Panther takes a deep breath and he quietly counts to three. " Then all of a sudden, Justin is standing there in his own form; and he looks around the room, and feels a little lightheaded because everything seems to be spinning.

Then Sly reminds him to breathe and relax into the breath, then quietly mentions to Justin,' just sit down really slow for a minute and acknowledge the things that have taken place. Sly then watches as Justin looks around the room, trying to find Panther Struts, and he couldn't find Panther.

Sly recognizes that Justin looks perplexed, and whispered to him and said, "It's okay, just feel and connect to your breathing through your heart. I will share with you what happened, just relax and take another deep breath, as I quietly finish up with Sammie, said Sly.

Justin listens and relaxes into his breathing and starts to feel better; then he glances at Sly and smiles, then telepathically said to Sly, 'I'm ok. Justin then notices Sammie picking up her crystals, and heard her say to Sly,' I feel better and aligned, through my energy, now.

Sly nods and agrees with Sammie and senses she's connected. Sammie mentions to Sly that she feels warm and bubbly inside; and smiled.

Sly could feel the excitement rising up through his heart chakra, because he knows the pink tourmaline helped Sammie's heart, a lot. Then he reminds Sammie telepathically, to work with her agate again; and that she could share more about the crystals, when she has time in the next class.

Sammie smiled and agreed with Sly as she felt proud and happy; as she held her crystals like they were her babies. SpiderBoy then gazes over at Justin and telepathically says to him, "oh hello, Panther Struts."

Justin looks around to see where Panther was, and couldn't see panther anywhere, and he looks at Sly bewildered and whispers, "well, I don't see panther, where did he go?"

Sly looked at Justin and smiled and telepathically said to him, "you are Panther Struts." Within that moment, Justin bit his tongue and said, "Me?" Sly just nodded and said happily, "yes, you are."

Justin then touched his hands, arms and legs; and his entire body, and then he shouts, "I don't see him, and I only see me." Then Sly immediately shares, "you're learning.

In our next class, I will show you how to see yourself; as you shape-shift.

As you practice shape shifting, you will acknowledge the powerful tool you have as a cat." Justin smiled the biggest grin that Sly had ever seen on Justin's face and could see he was so happy.

Sly said, "Take a deep breath Sammie, and bring your hands to your heart; and really thank yourself, for connecting to your crystals.

Sly then glances at Justin and reminds him to say,' thank you for connecting to Panther Struts." Then Sly peeks down into himself and acknowledges Spider Boy, and whispers 'thank you' to himself.

The next thing you know, Sly is bowing and honoring the sacred energies, they just worked with, by saying,' thank you spirits'. Both Sammie and Justin could sense Sly's energy was grateful.

At that moment they all telepathically thanked all guides and relatives, including Sly's helpers, 'the pixies'. As everyone was giving their thanks for the wonderful day; all the spirits were smiling and their energy was dissipating; as they left the room.

Sammie got up and was all excited as she stared at Justin and said, "You're just great. Look at all the wonderful things you did today. It's nice to see you, Panther Struts."

Sammie looked at Justin's right and left side, and she stared right into him, and Justin started to laugh, and said to Sammie, "You can see me?"

Sammie laughed and said "yes", and she winked at him.

Sly felt good, he had a decent day with the kids, and then he telepathically said to the kids, "Well, I must go and train, I will talk to you kids later;

'Please enjoy the day. 'Somewhere on StarDrome you will do all the wonderful things that you're meant to do. Through practice, with your crystals Sammie, you'll be amazing.

'Justin, you can also practice shape shifting as Panther Struts, and you'll be fascinated by who you become.' Until we meet again, this week.

"Blessings," whispered Sly, then Sammie and Justin gave him a hug and ran out of the room, happy. They were both excited about their next meeting with Sly, as they waved good bye...

Sly prepared the room for others, as it was important for all mentor's to cleanse the energy after each teaching. Sly remembers trying to cleanse the room as SpiderBoy; but it didn't work because he got everything sticky.

6

Shape Shifters Gather

Mel, Mazie, Luna and Jamie

Two years have passed; and time is going by very quickly. SpiderBoy is now 14 years old and acknowledges that he doesn't have a lot of time to learn the things that he desires. Then he can teach the younger cells, including Sammie and Justin.

Sly is aware that Luna is approaching her womanhood, she's 15 years old, but these years wouldn't of meant anything on another planet. But now in the new world, no cell soul can attach to age or numbers; all they can do is go by their wisdom.

This is how the masters determine how old a cell soul is, and how many journeys each cell had; before arriving on StarDrome. Recently SpiderBoy had a visitation from his mother in spirit, an apparition.

Some cells might call it that, but Sly knew that the apparition was his mother; and he chose not to speak or think very little about the episode. He clearly remembers though, what his mother said; as he's getting older he knows he won't forget such sacred messages.

Sly remembers that day, when his mother appeared to him and said,' Sly, one of the spots on your back, is going to release poisonous venom'. But, Sly was already learning how to use his webs, so he just listened to what his mother shared to him…within that moment his thoughts went back to Master and StarDrome.

Then Sly got lost in his thoughts…' Master Shade has given them a place where they can learn; and practice outside. Then he smiles and thinks about the time he was practicing outside… hanging on the trees; and using his webs.

But then Sly chuckles to himself, because he got stuck in his own webs a few times; and he knows that his webs are strong. Sly realizes that his webs can hold a lot of energy; and his webs can bound any prey, for some time.

Sly appreciates that his students are doing well, as Sammie's five and Justin is eight now. Sly is happy to know that Justin can shape-shift into Panther Struts; quite easily.

Plus, Sammie is working with her crystals and has accessed some new doorways, and she's learning about how portals work. SpiderBoy is aware that Sammie has been visiting different planes of energy; with Master Shade. Master mentioned to SpiderBoy that Sammie has grown to understand the teachings; through his direction as well.

Sly then remembers what Master Silver Cloud said to him the other day; 'Justin is growing into a fine young man, thanks to your teachings as well'.

Sly then smiles to himself and gathers his thoughts; and is quite pleased with the both of them. Sly then thanked himself for being a great mentor, as everyone is learning so quickly.

Sly shakes his head, takes a deep breath as he looking forward to connecting with the mentors. In the last meeting Master Shade did share that certain mentors weren't present because they were busy.

Today is the day to meet with them and sit in a wonderful energy and shape shift. Sly then prepares himself for the meeting and clears his thoughts, so he is ready to work with Mel who is 21 now. Mel is Gorilla Walks; and he is full of wisdom, from what Sly can tell.

Sly acknowledges whatever he needs, he can ask Gorilla Walks. Sly remembers Gorilla Walks said he would sit and quietly work with him, as long as the teachings are needed. Mel will let him know telepathically anytime, and to Sly, Gorilla Walks feels like the protector.

Not just to him, but to the rest of the crew, the rest of the mentors. Within that moment, it was kind of interesting for Sly. He starting chuckling to himself, when Gorilla Walks first turned blue, and he wasn't supposed to turn blue, but he did.

Sly was thinking about the time Mel got caught up in some of the energy that Mazie was throwing around, as she is Flower Power. As you know, she can camouflage herself, to match any terrain, plus she also releases deadly pollen. Mel was teaching her a few things and Mazie kind of got upset; and she aimed her flower petals at Mel, and he got some blue dust on him.

Mel wasn't really laughing about it, as he heard Sly's thoughts,' he quietly said to Sly, "my mother came to see me too. In my dreams and visions, I should add, she also mentioned to me; I was also the keeper of the books; for the rock people."

Then Mel looked down, away from Sly's eyes and even shared more, about his strange visit; and said, "On maybe one or two occasions, I got to go with my mom and sit down by the water.

Then Mel smiles and whispers that it was close to where Sly worked with the water beings. Sly was happy listening to what Mel was sharing, and listened closely as Mel continued.

'My mom looked so beautiful in her pink cotton dress.' Then she showed me the things that I needed to learn; 'said Mel. Plus, the things my mother was sharing will help me through my growth; so I can better understand myself.' As Gorilla Walks, I carry a lot of responsibility, as all of us mentors have our responsibilities.'

Not just for our own power, but for the powers of the cells we are teaching. It's for the young ones, the little ones as they will be following us, and they look up to us." Then Mel smiles and glances at Sly and proceeds to share more... Then Gorilla Walks' said that his mother also reminded him to prepare; and to always protect each other and to keep all eyes open.

Mel told Sly that he felt good with that, but Mel knew that he shape shifts into' Gorilla Walks' quite good. Plus, he confined in Sly that he wouldn't change that at all; and he knows that his strength will come in handy one day, as it will help others.

Gorilla Walks mentioned to Sly that he felt kind of uneasy, after the visit with his mother. Then he just stared at the ground, and smiled at Sly and said we all have our own truth, right? Then he added one more thing, "She didn't completely tell me everything," he said. "But I sensed that there was something that she didn't share."

Sly whispered to Mel, 'everything in its time, right. There are some things my parents still need to share; but 'trust' all things will come. Then Sly realizes with in that moment; within his thoughts, that his father was quiet, too.

Sly remembers seeing his father quietly standing behind his mother; when he was talking to him. Sly then shakes his head, and try's to quiet his thoughts, but Mel is very strong telepathically and continues sharing his thoughts, with Sly. Mel goes back to his memories and remembers the rocks; the old ancient ones.

Mel thinks of one memory in particular about grandfather, Rock of Ages. This grandfather rock carries many imprints and stories through time, and mentioned telepathically to Gorilla Walks that he already seen them coming to StarDrome; for a long time.

Plus, grandfather was aware of all the other cells that came in their pods, to StarDrome. They were all going to come and stay on StarDrome and co-create a new earth.

Well this surprised Mel, that's why he had to share his thoughts with Sly. Suddenly, it was quiet in Sly's mind, and then he heard Mel say quietly,' it kind of makes sense, what the old Rock of Ages shared;' because he has the gift of prophecy.

Then Sly shares with Mel that he agrees, because some things we can't explain, but just know. Then Mel thanked Sly for listening and said,' there is still lots of other things that he didn't share yet; because grandfather and I went deep into the taverns.

Then Sly had to remind both of them to take a deep breath and relax, while he went for a walk. Mel agreed and Sly could sense him relax, which was good for both of them. Within that second, sly reminded Mel to breathe, he continued sharing again and said,' 'There are places where people probably don't go, to learn.

Mel said quietly to Sly, "we are so blessed to be learning from the old ones, these ancient teachers; they have been through so many journeys. They are aware of so many things; and do you realize", he said telepathically to SpiderBoy, "That they could see us, before we even knew we were coming here, they could hear us.

Those old grandfather rocks, they are actually in tune." Then Sly said, yes' to Mel and mentioned that he would be seeing him soon. Then Sly shook his head once again, and took a deep breath and left to go meet Mel; he was excited about shape shifting with Gorilla Walks.

Sly felt great connecting with everyone telepathically, as he just did with gorilla Walks; then smiled to himself. It didn't take both boys too long to connect and work with some energy in nature; there was this perfect place on StarDrome they both loved.

The day was warm and the cabbage trees were strong and StarDrome was coming to life with all the wonderful energies; that every cell soul brought to the planet. SpiderBoy could see Mel practicing and warming up, and then he felt Mel telepathically notice him coming.

Mel quietly said to Sly, "we are going to be learning more, did you know that something big is going to happen?' You mark my words", he said to SpiderBoy. "I just don't know what it is, but it's going to be huge." Then Mel shape shifted into Gorilla Walks.

At that point, Sly watched Mel shift and noticed he was getting faster and now he sat there collectively listening; to Gorilla Walks share his wisdom. Sly put his hand on his shoulder and said to Mel, 'you are a very strong teacher too.

At that point, sly shape shifts into SpiderBoy; and whispered to Mel, 'you know, I acknowledge that you are on StarDrome to protect us, but you are also a protector to the gate. It is the doorway to where the rock people are, and they will always guide you;' as, you carry the gift of prophecy.

Then he reminded Mel, remember to breathe through all of this. "Set some of that knowledge beside you; so you can choose to look at later, because sometimes knowledge comes to us very quick.

Sometimes there's so much information coming to us, at the speed of light. But we will learn to decipher things through our wisdom, since we just need that extra time," articulates Sly, "and occasionally we get those answers later."

Gorilla Walks took a deep breath of fresh air and shook his head, and telepathically believed what SpiderBoy was sharing, "You are correct. But I will let you know if I feel or sense anything else." mentioned Gorilla Walks.

Then Mel looked up at Sly and said to him again, "just go do what you must and I will gladly let you know if anything changes." Then Mel states that he has a couple of students that he's working with as well.

Apparently, through Spider Boys understanding, from what Gorilla Walks was sharing; he felt that they couldn't share what they were teaching their students, to anyone. But out of strict confidence they both knew they had to be careful about what they shared," So, SpiderBoy agreed with what Gorilla Walks just said.

Sly shook his head and thought "Yes you are correct, "It is important to protect and keep our young ones safe, with their gifts." Sly then telepathically mentioned to Gorilla Walks, 'It's impossible to keep our thoughts clear and if there's anything in strict confidence that we need to share with anyone or with each other', then we meet in the green room.

Sly liked the green room because it was his favorite color, emerald green, but he never told anybody that. Well, Mel kind of knows now because he heard Sly's thoughts.

Then he quietly says to Mel, "Yes. We will meet in the green room, which is really the emerald room, and this is where we can share quietly the things that we want to keep sacred."

Mel then bows his head in respect and stepped back, then mentioned to SpiderBoy,' he must go and work with his two students, because there are some teachings that they need to take in today.

Sly nodded and thanked Gorilla Walks for the things that he shared earlier, as Mel proceeded to leave. SpiderBoy then observed how much Mel had grown, and how wise he's becoming.

Then SpiderBoy smiled and continued with his day. But, he couldn't stop thinking how he witnessed Mel's colors deepening and becoming stronger; when he shifts his energy.

Sly could see the deep blues through the black in his fur, and how the black was shiny like charcoal. Sly was feeling quite impressed with Gorilla Walks in that moment and trusts him, and that felt good in his heart.

Then Sly also senses telepathically that Gorilla Walks connected to his energy too; He felt the same way as he picked up on Sly's thoughts. Sly, then brings his hands to his heart and concentrates on the spirit of energy being received, because everyone was taught to honor the spirit of energy through all thought and action.

It was practice for every cell soul on StarDrome, not to think or do anything negative. As Sly went on his way, he walks past the 'Trees of Life' where the 'Golden Genie' sits and Sly knew he needed to keep his thoughts clear, as the Trees would show the Golden Genie the energy of thought and action, of every cell soul.

This is how the Masters would acknowledge who was having difficulty with the lessons being taught. No one could look at the Golden Genie, because he had the 'gift' to erase any cells memory and they would need to start learning from scratch again; or be sent to work in the salt mines.

If anyone was sent to the salt mines, then they would be of human form again; with no memories of StarDrome, but with their own realities that they created beforehand. Sly didn't know how many cells were there, but he does recognize he wouldn't be one of them.

Apparently, the Old Ancient knows why this one cell soul was turned into a Golden Genie; it's all written in the Book of Truth'. Then Sly gives his head a shake to clear his mind, as he hears a familiar laugh; it was Luna's.

The day was still young and Sly could see that Luna was growing into a wonderful, beautiful woman, and then he noticed she was doing some work with Jamie.

Because Sly could also hear Jamie's voice, as they were both laughing and Sly thought to himself in that moment, "Ok, that is what girls do, they come together, right? Sly then was trying to reassure himself that Luna missed him too.

Through Sly's thoughts, it just seemed that they're having a great time without him. But, he recognized that they were focusing their energy on what they needed to learn, through their exercises.

It wasn't that Luna was ignoring him; it was something that Sly had to acknowledge about his own emotions; plus it was something that he felt for some time. Sly knew he had to let go of any emotions around jealousy.

They're very close in age anyway, because Luna just turned 15, and quietly Sly would refer to her; as his flower girl. But, he didn't want Mazie to hear him, because she was Flower Power.

But, in his way, Luna was in his heart. Jamie, she's 6 years old, and she's quite interesting too, because she's Silver Fish. Sly senses as he walks towards them, that Jamie could slip into any place and hide.

Sly then said to Luna, "Jamie can go between any of those trees, even into our labyrinth, and she probably can hide very well." Then he smiles at both of them and he's thinking to himself,' it's kind of cute.'

He lets them continue with their lessons, as he quietly walks by, trying not to be to conspicuous. He notices Luna's red hair, blowing in the breeze. Sly could feel her connect to him energetically, and he quietly keeps that connection to himself, and just wished them both a good day.

Within that moment, Luna telepathically sent some wonderful energy his way and he remembers, Luna's energy, is the speed of light. Because she is Swift One and her powers are getting stronger and faster each time they connect.

Sly was so involved in the energy that Luna sent him; he fell to his feet and realized he tripped over Cora. Cora then proceeds to tell Sly, that he must help her pick up all the nuts and fruit she just dropped. Cora is one of the leaders of the squirrel families and she gathers the things needed for the tables; before everyone feasts.

Sly, apologized to Cora many times, but she chose's not to listen to him, because she's upset that she must go and clean the fruit and nuts, again.

Then Cora hurriedly picks up her baskets and leaves Sly there on his knees before he could notice she was gone; he was thinking of Luna, again. Sly knew Luna wasn't energetically whacking him, she was just sending him some good vibes.

Luna didn't realize how fast she could send energy. Until, she telepathically sent that energy Sly's way. Luna chuckled to herself and continued to work with Jamie. Sly recognized he was learning how to be aware and watch everything in his circles.

Sly sat there for a few seconds longer on his knees, and then he decided to shape-shift into SpiderBoy. As SpiderBoy his colors were red and black, and he took up a lot of space, as a spider. Then he proceeded to leap up to the top of the cabbage trees and he was looking down into the labyrinth.

Some cells could call this labyrinth a maze, but from what Master Shade called it, it was a magical labyrinth. It was energetically designed in a different way, with Hairy Trolls guarding the doorways. The only way through was by gifting them golden coins.

These coins were brought from the old world by Master Shade and the parents and guardians of each cell soul. The trolls could telepathically alter the thoughts temporarily to get more coins; because the cells won't remember gifting them a coin already.

SpiderBoy knew as Luna did, that the trolls couldn't trick them anymore, as they were too aware and would move their gold coins through telekinesis energy. Then this would keep the trolls preoccupied so they could use the maze. SpiderBoy liked to look down into the maze, to where Luna and Jamie were.

SpiderBoy could see where Jamie was hiding, because remember she could slide and fit into anything. So what SpiderBoy did in that moment was, he went down from the cabbage trees on his webs and took his little leg off and set it causally down where Jamie was, as a joke.

Then SpiderBoy gave Jamie a little push, and then all of a sudden, Jamie shape shifted into Silver Fish and flew right out into the open; Just, prior to Luna walking right toward that spot she smiled and was trying hard to hold her expression.

Jamie looked mesmerized and looked up at Luna and she said, "I don't know how that happened!" then they both felt SpiderBoy looking down at them, and they looked up with big eyes.

They saw SpiderBoy's red and black body run up the web, as fast as he could; then they both tuned in telepathically and told SpiderBoy to get out of their space and out of the labyrinth and quit bugging them.

SpiderBoy felt both their energies with such power. He felt the energy in his templates, and he tried to get out of there but he fell off his web, and landed on his back.

Now Sly realized to himself, it's not a good thing for a spider to land on its back, it's tricky because you've got to maneuver your body around to get back up.

So he quietly tried to get back up, so he wouldn't bring any attention to himself. But, it was impossible for SpiderBoy to be quiet because he was so big, and he was wrestling with the cabbage trees, as he got his webs in everything.

Then Luna and Jamie started sneaking around the area where SpiderBoy fell and Luna poked her head out of the bushes glancing at SpiderBoy trying so desperately to get up. After that, Jamie starting laughing when she looked at SpiderBoy, and said to him quite calmly, "So you think you can trick us, and sit there quietly on your web; and we wouldn't see you?

SpiderBoy quietly whispers to both of them, "Can you two, please help me get up?" The girls laughed and SpiderBoy heard Jamie laughing so hard. He glances her way and she was shape shifting in and out as Silver Fish.

SpiderBoy could see her blue flecks, and noticed how beautiful they looked; and they were mixed with the silver energy that ran down her back. Jamie noticed in that moment how SpiderBoy was staring at her, and she felt her eyes do something funny.

Then she quit laughing and noticed Luna was still laughing, as she stared at SpiderBoy. Then Luna smiles and telepathically said to Sly, "Do you want any help?" then she giggles again.

At that point Luna turned back to look at Jamie, as she wondered why Jamie was so quiet. All of a sudden Luna stopped giggling and saw Jamie cleaning herself off, as she had twigs, grass and other things on her.

Unexpectedly, SpiderBoy was hanging upside down, above them and said; "Is everything all right? How come you guys aren't laughing anymore? Are you going to help me get up? Is there something wrong?" then SpiderBoy laughed.

Luna looked at SpiderBoy and said, "What's the matter with you? "You startled us". Then Jamie added to the conversation, "I really think my eyes are opening up, and remember how Master Shade said a long time ago, that my eyes could freeze anything, through my gaze? Well look at this."

105

SpiderBoy and Luna watched, as Jamie turned to her left and she focused on the cabbage trees in front of her. Then all of a sudden to their amazement, Luna and Sly noticed one of cabbage trees turned frosty and had tinges of silver. Luna then decided to walk over to the tree, because she heard it crying; and one of the branches of the cabbage tree broke in half.

Then SpiderBoy mentioned to Silver Fish that she had to nurse that tree back to health. Master Shade mentioned one time, that the cabbage trees cry until healed. But, no one knows how long the trees cry, it's up to each individual tree and its healer.

Luna then gave the tree some healing through her energy and said, "Oh my God! Jamie's got her sight. She's freezing everything into ice." Everyone felt excited; and then SpiderBoy said something, while he hung upside down, "Um it would be nice if you two could help me get down, as I'm stuck in my webs again.

'Then I could really hear and see what you two are talking about." Thanks! Sly telepathically reminded Jamie,' don't gaze at me, because I don't want to be a frozen spider."

Sly tried to be humorous, then Luna and Jamie came running over to untangle him, and Luna whispered, "Well if you get any bigger, there's no way that I'm going to be able to help you get up. 'This is why you need to practice some more, SpiderBoy; that's why you've got two legs." And Luna untangled the webbing from his legs.

SpiderBoy considered what Luna just said, and frowned; then he alleged, "Oh yeah, sure,' Mom." Both girls helped SpiderBoy get down, and right away SpiderBoy started straightening out his back, and the girls could hear his bones click and clack.

They could see how big SpiderBoy was getting, as he towered over them. Then SpiderBoy said to Jamie, "Congratulations, Silver Fish, you know how to freeze'. SpiderBoy smiles easily, and reminds her to only use her gifts, on enemies.

Sly also adds,' Even though we don't have enemies on StarDrome, we're on a new planet. Jamie,' your gifts are only there, just in case; just like me," said SpiderBoy. "I have poisonous venom."

At that point, Luna observed Sly and agreed they all need to be aware of what they are doing, respectively, for each other. Because, now they must figure out how to heal these trees that are crying… Luna then mentions to SpiderBoy,' You do have poisonous venom'; because Master Shade shared this knowledge in class, right?!

"Well really, I first found this out from my mom, because she came to visit me, too." Luna and Jamie looked at SpiderBoy and said quietly, "You have poisonous venom?" "Well apparently, I guess I could kill. Well, I don't like that word, but I guess I could kill if I need to.

Let's just say, I can poison someone." Both girls looked at him and said, "Whoa. Everybody's getting so strong."

"Sh. Said SpiderBoy, the Golden Genie is nearby and we need to be careful thinking and sharing, because sometimes we don't know whose listening.

"Oh," said Luna and Jamie. "Ok." Remember, nothing is hidden on StarDrome; we all share our gifts here, to assist this planet. "Well," Jamie said to Luna, "we better get back to what we were doing because we need to have these lessons finished; before Master Shade meets with us later. Luna nodded and said,' and apparently we've still got to count all the spirit rocks with Mel that are still there.

Plus, we need to let Master Shade know, what each rock represents. Remember, Jamie?" Jamie casually said,' I just about forgot about that, thanks for reminding me. Luna knew Jamie was truthful because she was strong in her telepathic energy and Luna then quietly whispered to Jamie, "Ok, just one second.

I'm just going to quickly say bye to Sly." Then she marched over to SpiderBoy and gave him a kiss on his right cheek. Luna then whispered softly to him, "Take care and don't forget to learn how to get up because we're not going to be there all the time to help."

Then she smiled and strolled away while Sly looked at them as they were leaving and quietly smiled and thought "Wow. This made my day." Sly was happy and he smiled and walked away.

Everything on StarDrome was humming and growing, Sly could sense the strong magnificent energies of the mentors and teachers, and he smiled again. As he continued on his way, Sly could hear things happening from a mile away.

He realized his spider senses were getting stronger and he could hear Master Shade speaking with other students. Master Shade was working with a couple of mentors; one was Star, she is 8 yrs. old now, well she would have just turned 8, Sly thought to himself.

As Sly continued listening, he thought to himself "Ok, I know that other voice. It's George's voice. Oh," he says to himself quietly. "George is 12 now, Wow! This is kind of interesting; George and Star are working together.' I would love to work with them.

Well, we all get our chances. We're all training with Master Silver Cloud; and there's an Old Teacher we're going to meet next week. Sly realizes he's deep in thought... The Old Teacher comes from the South of StarDrome; his name is 'Monkey Dances'.

Well, he has some kind of special pod that he travels in, and for some reason that pod doesn't shrink. It would be very interesting to work with him because he's very old and wise.

Sly thought to himself, "well, old teacher, old ancient. Old pod, well this is kind of cool".

Sly then decided to listen some more and he knew he wasn't supposed to be eavesdropping. But he lent his ear to the conversations between Master Silver Cloud and Starfish.

All of a sudden, Sly could hear this sound in his ear, the ringing wouldn't stop. The ringing was getting louder and he tried to cover his ear, he shape-shifted back into himself, as Sly, and he couldn't stop the ringing.

Then, Sly heard this loud demanding thought in his head and it said, "Butt out." And he knew who that was, it was Maser Silver Cloud. He had to remind sly, "mind your own business."

Sly realized immediately, he better pull his energy back. As he proceeded to do this; he observed all the purples, blues and greens in his energy coming back into his aura; until he was grounded again.

Sly felt centered again and the big bang in his head went away. Plus, the ringing in his ear was gone, as he stood there. Then thought to himself, "Interesting. We're all very strong, very gifted." I will definitely not tune in again, to private conversations; then he smiled to himself.

Sly realized he better listen to Master Silver Cloud, because when Master says something, we better choose to listen. That's one of my things, I'm learning to listen."

Sly quietly goes back to the healing room because he has some work to attend to, as well as collect his tools.

Sly chooses to shape-shift into SpiderBoy, because he can move quicker and cover more terrain. On his way back, SpiderBoy chooses to go down by the water and sit there and connect with the water beings again.

Sly could feel the emotion of sadness as he connected; there was still a lot of work to be completed with the water. As Sly looks around, he comes to terms with all the work that has to be done with the land, yet.

Sly honored the water beings, as they were doing considerable work to bring balance to this land.

Sly decided to assist somehow again, as the water beings knew Sly was destined to take care of the water; as well as others that were on StarDrome.

He was required to lend a hand with the ground, so he grabbed some tools and went to assist the earth keepers. Sly noticed there wasn't that many earth keepers, they were digging, planting and doing many things to bring fruition to StarDrome.

Sly felt the rays of the sun were too hot; they could only plant at certain places, where the cabbage trees were. The cactus loved the hot sun, the earth keepers were being warned, and they were still learning to protect themselves from the sun.

Sly could tell they needed some rest, and probably desired some water. Sly took his water pouch off his shoulder and went over to where they were, and shared the water.

Sly quietly asked the water beings to bless the earth keepers, so that they could feel good. Through Spider Boy's intentions, he made sure to ask the water beings to keep them strong, from inside out, because we need those earth keepers.

Sly knew deep down inside, the earth keepers played a vital role on StarDrome, because they were assigned certain tasks. He could see their energies changing, as they shifted into their protective shields. Sly watched as the earth keepers danced in their wonderful energy.

Sly watched as all that beautiful dancing energy went directly into the earth and created a magical ray of blues and greens. It was a beautiful sight to see, as Sly could feel StarDrome getting nurtured.

This new world required what she was receiving; this beautiful love and light energy. SpiderBoy felt good with what the earth keepers were doing, and he felt very connected throughout his body. Sly was witnessing first hand, things come to life in the ground again and the earth keepers were very humbled by what he'd done.

They gave Sly a gift and thanked him for being there and presenting his energy to them. It then made sense to Sly the importance of everyone coming together, as a collective.

The earth keepers were proud to work with SpiderBoy. Even though they didn't see him shape-shift, they understood who he was. Sly felt good and thanked the water beings for their support.

He knew wherever they went; they would create new life-force. Sly could sense the water beings were happy. The ground was waking up and refurbishing StarDrome once again.

The earth keepers could see all her greens, blues and yellows. It was interesting how colorful StarDrome looked. There was some harvest that needed to be picked, but Sly left that alone.

Because, that wasn't his area of work at this time; there were other little helpers that could assist as well. Sly had to remind himself once again,' balance'. StarDrome had those beings that assist them through the ground, and he noticed from deep down inside the earth; they would come and help.

Somewhere in the ground they're connected to the butterfly kingdom. Master Shade shared that the butterflies only come out after a torrential rain, as StarDrome receives rain every 100 light years.

The butterflies are different on StarDrome, they are purple and brown with a white stripe down their back; these ones are the male species. Apparently, from what the masters' claim, there are only 3 clear white butterflies, these are the only females.

The butterflies only last for a few days, then die, but they enhance the energy of the 'Purple Suede', Sly remembers the talk that Master Silver Cloud gave; he shared a little about the 'Purple Suede'.

Master said that the Purple Suede only grows once, but it has wonderful healing agents, so it was imperative that everything aligned on StarDrome.

This was another reason why every cell soul had a responsibility, because if one thing wasn't in sync; then all would go wrong. Those things that master shared, helped Sly feel at ease because he knew in this new world everyone was interconnected.

Everyone helped everyone; it was the law or agreements all cells said,' yes' to. Each group had a different task to complete, and all that energy was interconnected on StarDrome.

Everyone knew telepathically, if something was out, then they would align and reconnect their energies. Each cell was taught the importance of balance on StarDrome, not just for night but for day as well.

Sly telepathically asked if the earth keepers needed anything else, and they indicated gratitude to him. Sly waved gratitude back, and then he gathered up his pouch and tools then headed back to the healing room.

Sly felt privileged, he liked this new world. Within that moment, Sly recognized the importance of everyone coming together. Just as he knew earlier that Tiger Running was good, too.

He trusted George and all the things that he could do.

Sly knew that Tiger Running could leap and capture any prey, and he knows that George has been practicing every day.

Master Shade had given him a place that he could practice and he's getting faster now, he's a big cat. Sly thought, at least 10 feet in length. Sly could notice Tiger's eye tooth is out now, but he's still learning how to use it.

Master Shade said it would take some time to master, because the tooth has to be mature to release any kind of toxin.

But that's not what the mentors were focused on, as Master Shade mentioned in the teachings, we are here to learn. To honor our intuition, gifts and power, for the positive, not the wrong.

Master Shade shared some teachings about the spirit of StarDrome; she went through war and negative energy already. He mentioned that as cell souls we choose StarDrome for healing and positive flow.

If any cell choses to take on negative energy or thoughts, it would be through the old emotions; that are written in the Book of Truth.

All the masters know that these old emotions, if not healed and forgiven; could create war, such as it was done on old earth.

But the wrong was there, not on StarDrome because that is why certain cells were chosen. But it took some practice for Tiger Running to chew only on his right side. All of us on StarDrome sent him some healing energy so he could adapt to this new way of eating.

Tiger knew it was difficult because cats like to eat with all teeth. Then he growled, and let out a great big sigh, and starting walking back to the center of StarDrome with Sly. They ran into Star again, and she whispered to SpiderBoy, "I can slowly let go of toxins now."

Sly smiled and said, "Good. Remember, we need to keep it silent. Silent power is the key, remember? It's good for all of us to know and understand our gifts.

But we only share our gifts, with the strictest confidence. Sly also mentioned to Star, he saw Gorilla Walks and said,' we can meet in the emerald room', that's where any of us can share. In the emerald room we can come together as a group or individually, to share because nothing can be heard in the Green Room.

Then Sly whispers to Star,' so if anyone wants to meet, we can; please let Luna know this, too. She is working with Jamie, and it would be a good reminder for both of them. Master Shade said we could post a reminder on the door, if anybody wants to meet with him or other mentors, send it out telepathically so that everyone knows the time and place for that meeting."

Starfish nodded and whispered, "OK", and she scurried off. Sly knew that it was a good day, because he could feel the magic in the air, and things were coming to life on StarDrome.

There were so many things to be grateful for, with all the different rooms and space on StarDrome. Sly could sense that StarDrome is going to be a fascinating place. Sly gets all excited because he gets to work with Mazie and Alex, tomorrow.

Mazie is 18 and Alex is 13 now, Sly is quite pleased because Mazie is Flower Power, and a few of them, will be working in the terrain. 'Mazie gets to camouflage herself, and we get to find her'; Sly smiled and said to George,' to bad you're busy tomorrow, or you could come out for the day!'

Then Sly mentioned to George that they will also get to check and see if Mazie is re-leasing any pollen yet. Then Sly chuckled and said,' not so that we turn blue, and Mazie would probably laugh about that, because it already happened to Mel.

Then George and Sly laughed as they noticed Alex practicing his lessons and preparing for tomorrow, as well. George then asked Sly, "will Alex go down to the terrain with you guys tomorrow?'

Sly nodded and said,' Alex will be down at the water this time tomorrow, and he'll have a beautiful place to work as Jelly Stinks.

Master Shade shared with us, that Alex must practice some more, changing into his lime green color. Master also mentioned, to make sure not too many cells are around, because Jelly Stinks emits a dangerous gas.

Then there was some silence between both boys and Sly said,' there is a lot of things that we're going to be doing, and it will be interesting.

George nodded and agreed with Sly; then Sly mentioned,' we just need to remind Alex to stay in the water during the day, and come out at night only. But Jelly Stinks can protect the ones at night, from the spirits or energies that is out there.

Because the spirits that exterminated our parents can't hurt him, he's immune to that.' So that helps Alex a lot' and it works out well, from what Master Shade said. Sly is signing off for the day, and waved good bye to George so he could go get something to eat.

Sly then mentioned to George,' hurry up, as everyone is sitting down for dinner, and we're at the round table. George nodded and Sly hurriedly mentioned,' it's in the round room, and everybody likes the idea of being at a round table in a round room.

Then George hurried off, as Sly was thinking about the creative energy involved in constructing the table; it can be made bigger, as we only add sections to it; so it opens up. It's resembles a large round puzzle piece and each piece is a different color; and holds a different vibration.

The vibration holds the energy of the mentor's day and lessons etc. The coolest thing is all the young souls sit in the center, as to protect them. The fairies were around the center pieces adding to the colors with Cora and her families.

Everyone had a special place around the table, and it never grew too small. All of the older souls were seated on the outside circles, to protect the masters. Then the ancients protected the masters, as StarDrome protected all inhabitants, as one unit.

Sly thought, when looking down at the round room as SpiderBoy, it looks like a spiral of energy within spirals of energy. With little spaces where each cell soul can come and go, as needed; so they don't disrupt anyone.

Sly felt his stomach growling and thought to himself and said,' Very good creative energy, so, until later. Thanks.

7

StarDrome's Secret

Exposed

StarDrome's energy has been increasing since the cell souls inhabited this new world. The mentors are becoming resilient as the parents and guardians are dying off. StarDrome has a few old teachers and ancient ones left to teach. All of these thoughts were pacing through Spider Boy's head and he was trying to keep his thoughts clear and positive.

This practice took place every day, by all the cell souls etc. Sly discerns that Luna, Mel, George and Mazie, and all of the mentors, have been working hard with their gifts. Through their intuition and visions, everyone can notice that they are becoming stronger.

Sly senses that he needs to meet with others, in the green room today. He acknowledges any meetings held, are in strict confidence. Then he agrees to meet with Mel, Max, Luna, and George. Energetically, it felt good for everyone wanting to attend because it was understandable why the mentors were required to share energies.

So quietly, telepathically, Sly indicates to Sammie and Justin that he'll see them later. Sammie and Justin were used to Sly and his teachings; so they were okay with what Sly suggested. They both honored the spirit of the lessons they received today, with Sly and thanked him.

Then they both smiled and waved, to let SpiderBoy know everything is Ok; as they close their energy for the day. Sly smiles and reminds both of them to keep busy with the lessons he taught them today because they're making great strides.

Sly felt like a new papa to the children. It reminded him how his mother and father would have taught him. Sly realized in that moment that he learned a lot in a short time while on StarDrome. He knows intuitively that his parents see him and can connect to him anytime.

Plus, it's reassuring knowing that he is being watched over, as are all cells on StarDrome. There are so many things to learn, beyond StarDrome; zones where other pods have set down. Cell souls on different planetary systems have set up residence… we only hear occasionally from them.

As, mentors we ask questions about the other kids, are they mentors; do they live similar to us on StarDrome? The masters chose to keep it quiet, as we can only imagine what's going on in their worlds.

When we come together in the green room as mentors, we set our intentions for all of them. We hope one day, we will learn more; Sly gives his head a shake once again, because he is full of fleeting thoughts, as he gets ready to go and meet the others.

Sly shakes his thoughts off, making sure he is clear as he gathers up his tools; and his journal. It isn't the Book of Truth because only the masters keep it sacred, for reasons. All of the mentors have sacred journals to keep track of their student's daily lessons.

Even with all the teachings taking place from the masters, the mentors have a sacred place to store the wisdom. This way it can be passed down to others, such as Sammie and Justin.

Every journal holds crucial information, but it is invisible to the human eye; only the mentors can read what's in the journals.

Sly smiles to himself, knowing that his sacred journal holds old wisdom and lessons. These lessons will carry on for centuries; as long as it remains in good hands. Each journal has a unique key with a different color and shape. Each specific key has been fastened with each mentor's DNA; no one else can gain access to the sacredness of the teachings, except the Old Ancient, called 'Silver Moon".

She holds all the sacred keys and can dissolve all other keys; if needed. Silver Moon has access to all the mentors' journals and keys on StarDrome.

It was designed that way, to protect the journals and keys; so the lessons aren't used against them for other purposes. The masters make sure everything is kept sacred; as the journals hold all wisdom from all mentors; and teachers before them.

Especially from old earth…When the journal is passed to a different mentor, a new key is made. The master who makes these keys is very ancient, he is known as 'Knightley'.

No one sees him unless they need a 'key'. Only Monkey Dances knows where to find him, this is how Knightley likes it, because he had enough of the old world frequency. Sly senses within his heart that Knightley could be more than 103 years old, but in spirit's time, add decades more.

Sly smiled again, feeling reassured that all things are protected and safe. Sly gets closer to the emerald room as he is busy in his thinking and realizes when all of them get together with their energies.

Wonderful things can happen, Sly can sense the excitement of coming together, and he knows in his heart that Luna is there already. He reminds himself to quiet his thoughts, so she doesn't pick up on anything, but only they are sharing as a group.

All he can do is smile, and chuckle, and send good vibes to Luna, without throwing his energy off. He then walks into the green room and prepares for the meeting, Mel mentioned a few things before they started about deep breathing.

Luna's very fast, even before shape-shifting into Swift One; he realizes that he'll get the opportunities to work with her in the next few weeks. This is where Sly knew he would be able to practice riding with her, as SpiderBoy.

Without falling off Luna's back; Sly chuckles to himself because it was practice keeping up with the energy and movement; as it is the speed of light. Any spider would have to hang on tight, but Sly knows he is getting better with his web.

Luna then looked up at Sly and noticed the biggest smile she ever saw on his face. It was ear to ear and then he winks at her; she turned a little red and focused her energy somewhere else. Sly chooses to position himself in a free spot, close to George and Max.

Luna mentions telepathically that Mazie is coming, and sly smiles knowing that it's a good thing. Then he mentions to Luna and Mel telepathically,' do we have any questions for Jamie, Alex, Clayton, and Lena?

And they weren't sure, at that point, as George entered the emerald room asking the same question. George could hear and relate to the energy in the room and he said,' Lena will be here shortly, she is finishing up with her students, Sylvie and Mark.

Who are 6 and 3 years old, the mentors knew Mark worked with the swimmer's energy. He connects to the water, but in a different way and shape-shifts into a shark. He likes to be called 'Blue' for short.

Mark can camouflage himself with the water and is very fast. Sly and Max knew that Lena's very proud of her students as well, and then Max mentions that Sylvie is growing stronger every day.

Her name is 'Spirit Hawk' she shape-shifts quite easily. Her beautiful song will pierce the drum of any ear; and to negative influences this could be death, to the hearing.

Then Lena walks in and reminds Sly and Max to share when she is in the room, not before. She gives them a hug and finds a spot in the room. All the mentors had amazing students, we all know this intuitively in our hearts. All our students will grow and become wiser and will have their own students to teach.

Jamie could feel the energy, as she approached the green room, and she decided to clean her energy off before she entered. As she was just out for a swim, and the other mentors will tell by her energy that she's depleted a little. Plus, Master Shade had worked with her well, as all the mentors know and understand that Master is very effective.

Sly is observing Jamie as she enters the room; he notices her silver color with blue flecks. To Sly her flecks were fading, this is how he knew her energy was tired, from what she's doing. Then he decides to help her ground her energy and Jamie smiles and she telepathically sends out a big Hi' to everyone.

Jamie is usually clear and abrupt in her energy and wants everybody to know that she's present; and she's aware of what's going on in the moment. Suddenly, she plops herself down beside Sly, on his right. This is where Sly sensed she was going to sit; sometimes Jamie would throw his thoughts off, but not too often.

Sly nods and Luna's chuckling, and Mazie's all excited as she comes into the green room too. She chooses to sit beside Luna, and the girls started speaking amongst themselves, through their thoughts.

They were trying to embarrass the young men that were present. All the boys didn't react, all they did was remind the girls to 'hush', because it was important to ground and get ready for the meeting. Then all the boys said together, "Let's breathe and bring our intentions into our hearts, so we can fill this emerald room with beautiful colors of energy."

Then the room grew quiet and Clayton was the last one to arrive and he apologized quickly because he was running behind. He mentioned the lessons took a bit longer, with his student Randy, who's 11.

Clayton mentioned to everyone, it still takes practice for Randy to shape-shift. He is a beautiful black stallion, very gracious and a quick thinker. I'm proud to say,' we all have amazing students'.

They are very strong and dedicated kids, just like us' and he smiled at everyone. Clayton quietly lets the other mentors know that he feels satisfied with everything he's teaching; and he is feeling good now.

Clayton is teaching two boys, the other boy is Scott. And he shape-shifts into a monkey, we call him Monkey Eyes, said Clayton. He can swing high and low, he's a master in the trees, and he can hide very well, Randy and Scott practice their lessons together closely.

Scott is 16, and then Mel quiets his thoughts, takes a deep breath and because he's the oldest one in the group, he reminds everyone to breathe and to relax. Then the others will have their opportunities to share when they choose, Clayton reminds everyone telepathically to clear their thoughts;

Clearing their minds of everything they were doing before they came to the emerald room; and just connect with your energy, through your heart and soul. Then he reminded everyone again, breathe, and feel your energy within your body through all your cellular levels.

Everyone felt connected and the energy in the room was spiraling with colors of green and blue, through everyone's vibration. Mel noticed as he was walking around the room, everyone had their eyes closed, with their palms on their knees.

All the mentors were grounding through their breathing as they were welcoming the new energy in StarDrome. They can see through their visions how much StarDrome had changed; she was becoming stronger and more compelling.

The energy vibrations are moving quickly and the energy emanates as a beautiful purple, blue, and green, with shades of red and yellow. These colors surrounded StarDrome's gardens and new crops.

There was golden energy streaming from the center of StarDrome with beautiful specks of white running through it; the visions were breathless to Mel as he watched and listened. He notices Clayton get up, to motion him to enjoy the meditation as well.

Mel then nods his head in favor and seats himself quietly and goes directly into his visions. Then Clayton walks around the room and he places his hands one at a time on each of the mentors left shoulder, and he starts to run energy and connect with each of them.

Clayton then proceeds to rejuvenate their systems completely, from head to toe. Then he takes a deep breath and he telepathically reminds everyone to breathe. He mentions to them that through their breathing; they are letting go of the sad and low vibrational energies.

They no longer need on this planet and now breathe in only the new high vibrational energies because these vitalities assist us here and it helps everything grow with speed and urgency. Everything is nurtured by that positive vibration, we all hold as cells.

Clayton then proceeds around the room once again and places his hand on everyone's shoulder until he's done running the energy. This way all the mentors will feel strong, connected, clear, and open telepathically.

In this way each mentor feels aligned mentally, emotionally, physically, and spiritually, and their thoughts are quiet. After that, Clayton notices what everyone is watching through their visions; and how each person relates to the things that they've been teaching to their students.

As they've been sharing visions and teachings with each other, assisting them so they can strengthen the things they each teach to the young ones. Everyone in the room could now feel and connect to the space, as the emerald room.

By feeling relaxed, fearless and content, Clayton then reminds everyone to breathe again, and then he motions Mel to come behind him, and place his right hand on everyone's right shoulder one more time.

Mel gets up and he follows Clayton as he is proceeding to finish his work; then Mel can sense the intense energies from each individual, in that moment he shape-shifts into Gorilla Walks.

Sly notices how deep the color blue is on Mel's fur, with the little flecks of black running through it. Sly does acknowledge that Mel is becoming older, and his color blue is enhancing.

Mel just heard what Sly was telepathically thinking and said, "Yes, you're correct to say that", and grinned at him. Then they both beckoned the same thoughts again,' to breathe', then all the mentors took a deep breath once again. Clayton is very strict in regards to the things he needs to do with everyone.

Then and there Clayton started to telepathically look at Luna with his eyes closed, indicating to her to increase her energy flow and shape-shift into Swift One. Then Luna was delighted to hear she could shape shift into Swift One, and shifted energy, resembling the wind.

Every mentor could individually sense her strength, poise and agility. Luna's energy was her strength, joy and enthusiasm, and Jamie telepathically mentions to Luna that her mane is getting really red and beautiful.

When Jamie was gazing at Swift One, her mane resembled the red flames of a burning fire, then Luna's big blue eyes look back at Jamie and she said, "thank you".

Jamie giggled when she realized Luna heard her thoughts; then Luna snickered as Jamie continued watching her prance, as Swift One. Luna danced around the room quickly, one minute she was beside Jamie and in the next moment she standing beside Mazie.

Everyone can feel Swift One's tresses and the gentleness of her cheek rubbing against them as she ran by; very quickly, delicately, as each mentor received the vibrations of strength and hope.

The energy of appreciation and hope could be felt by all the mentors in the room. Then Swift One casually walked by Sly and gave him, her little horse giggle, just to acknowledge Spider Boy once more. Luna did that gesture just then to let Sly know that she didn't forget about him; and she understands him.

Sly could also sense in that moment, Luna trusts that he'll wait for her; then Sly telepathically agreed with her as she walked around the room again and stood beside Mel, snorting down his back.

As the men were finishing up their healing work, Mazie stood up and she shape-shifted into a beautiful blue and purple flower. The shades were similar to her favorite flower, the violet.

Mazie was displaying her softness, color and boldness; she also sent out her energy so brightly into the room. As she always gives that energy of love to everyone she knows. Mazie feels satisfied that she could shape-shift and she knows that she is getting better with camouflaging herself.

Mazie was telepathically excited about sharing her visions about the terrain she had to practice in, with Master Shade. She was so happy because she beat Master Shade, he couldn't find her, as she camouflaged herself so well.

But then Mazie chucked to herself because Master Shade found her eventually, and what gave her away was the sweet scents that were coming from the pollen. Mazie was trying to quiet the flowers around her, but they kept talking…

Then Mazie smiled sincerely, and everyone smiled with her, because Master Shade would connect with the senses of sweetness, bitterness and whatever was in the energy around him. As, all the mentors knew he could shift into anything he chose...

Mazie felt fulfilled today as she quietly found herself a place to sit, in the far left side of the room. The room felt relaxed, as all the mentors shared their talents, lessons and journeys with each other.

George gets up and shape-shifts soundlessly and elegantly into Tiger Running; and everyone could see he's a beautiful big cat. He has an enormous body with tan brown fur and a black stripe, right down his back.

George decided to extent his body easily across the room and the mentors are surprised by his agility and strength. Tiger can't really run and leap today, the way he would like; but it suits him fine because he is still acquiring some teachings around honoring his female energy.

As he knows he can telepathically send this wonderful vision out in front of him, especially when he has limited space to work in because he enjoys leaping and running for miles.

George has memories of working with Master Shade, he smiles to himself and recalls when he first shape shifted; he felt so alive and ran for a mile...Master Shade had to send his helpers out to gather his energy, so he could be reminded about keeping his energy in his space (aura). Plus, Master Shade quietly reminded Tiger Running that he couldn't run astray.

George smiled as he shared that vision because he felt empowered by his name and realized through the teachings he had to stay aware of his surroundings. It wasn't easy to learn about the essence of his female side.

He then shook his head of his thoughts and indicated through his energy, with the others, that they could tune in and feel the strength and agility and honor the spirit of who they are as shape shifters.

Not just as a two legged, but as a four legged, winged and swimmers, the wonderful tools and gifts they all carried. George placed his left hand over his heart and he swore to be there for everyone, no matter what, we are all friends. He quietly found a discreet place to sit and share the energy of what he was feeling, the intensity of love and gratitude, with the others.

Within that moment, Clayton telepathically reminded everyone to 'breathe again. Lena got up, and she was going on 15 now, and she felt satisfied, vibrant and assured as she shape-shifted into Space Envy; she is reptilian.

Everyone was quite surprised by her spikes, as they arose out of her spine. They were longer and stronger, as they covered the length of her spine.

All of the mentors could feel every hair in the room stand up on end, on everyone, including Gorilla Walks. He was starting to feel a little itchy on the top of his head and behind his ears, but he knew it was good energy. It was a good vibration that Space Envy was sending out and everyone noticed.

Lena was sharing about her webbed feet and hands that they were becoming more profound and she decided to show them through her visions. She also shared all of the lessons she was learning, in and out of the water, and she was keeping her balance between both. Because, it was important for her to do so, as she likes to be in the water and on land.

Space Envy felt quite comfortable shape-shifting into a reptilian and she hasn't used her hypnosis yet , so she's practicing more and feels noble with what she's learning, one step at a time.

She reminds the other mentors,' we're all teachers to each other through our energy frequencies, and then smiled.

"One shift at a time," Lena declares. 'Take this from the old reptile, as there's a lot of wisdom here; and then she smirks and she brings a coolness of energy to everyone. The energy was felt by all the mentors, as it travelled into their aura.

Everyone in the room starts to feel content, calm, enlightened and embodied, within all the beautiful energy.

Clayton then reminds everyone to take a deep breath again, and then Alex quietly sits there in the sacred space, minding his own business, shape-shifting into Jelly Stinks.

Jelly Stinks didn't even say a word, he just started showing everyone in the emerald room what he was doing as he was proud of his lime green colors; and Alex mentioned telepathically to everyone, "I can glow in the dark."

Alex then, let out a little chuckle because he was so excited. Because this was something new that he had recognized a few days ago, he also mentioned to Master Shade that he could go out into the dark, and he wouldn't be harmed.

Within that moment Alex wished that he would have had that energy, that power, before his parents died. He wanted to be there, when Sly's parents died, but his energy and his power wasn't strong yet.

Alex likes glowing in the dark, plus he didn't have any dangerous gas that would cause choking or anything. But he is aware of his gift, and feels he wouldn't resist using it when he needs to.

Master Shade reminded everyone about their powers, when to use them and when not to; as all gifted cells live through unconditional love first.

Sly just looked up at Master Silver Cloud and nodded as did everyone in the room. It was respectable to be sitting in that sacred room together, as everybody's energy was felt because it was positive, kind and loving.

Star didn't make it to the emerald room today because she was busy with the rainbow cells. She was teaching the two younger ones, so they can better understand the teachings. The rainbow cells were being prepared for work with the elementals.

The rainbow cells work at a different speed; these two students of Star's are twins. They were born in their pod and they do things together as they share one link, a tail.

Star has been feeling overwhelmed with the twins, but it's conveying a lesson, that is decent. Star has noticed that the tail the twins share has a spike distended from the tip. There's a lethal poison in the spike, similar to the scorpion's venom. Sly recalls one of the kids from block D shape-shifts into a scorpion.

He believes his name is Scorpion Hits, but he's not definite on it. Master Shade also knows the importance of teaching the twins about their tail; as the twins will grow to acknowledge they are from a different species. It's written in the Book of Truth, how the twins were born out of experiments done to their mother…from the old world.

But Sly is aware that they'll all be meeting soon… and then Clayton reminds everybody to take a deep breath and he lets everyone know telepathically that their doing a great job teaching their students.

Master Shade agreed with Clayton and telepathically, said,' I'm pleased with all the things you all have been doing, as you've been responsible; not just with your students but with yourselves'.

'There's a lot of amazing things happening on StarDrome, "confirmed Master Shade. Then, Max mentions to Clayton that he wants to share as well. Then he decides to shape-shift into Lion Heart.

Clayton decided to shape-shift into Raven's Face, right after that and his wings were enormous. Master Shade could see how Clayton could move his wings close together.

Master knew that this took great discipline and discernment and was content on what he was witnessing. Raven showed everyone in the room how far he could stretch his wings and protect them.

He felt worthy, calm and every person in the emerald room could tell from his gaze, Raven was resilient. All of the mentors knew that good things were to come on StarDrome. Master Shade then proceeded to signal to Max and asked Lion Heart how his whiskers were doing.

Lion Heart became excited when Master Shade asked him this question; he then suddenly pulled out a couple of whiskers. Throwing one whisker left and the other right, and the whiskers moved through the energy in the room, circling all around and they landed on a gold plate.

Max starts to laugh, then abruptly understands he needs to discern and be responsible, but he also had a question running through his mind. 'Why did the whiskers land on a gold plate?'

Within that moment, Max glances at the gold plate and could see the poison coming out of the darts. Well, Max liked to call his whiskers darts, because they're strong and firm enough to be darts. He felt innocent in that moment and then mentioned to everyone to look at the gold plate.

Everyone gazed at the gold plate and saw a vision coming from the poison. The vision was of a terrifying moment yet to come, on StarDrome. Master Shade then lifted his hand and cleared the vision. He whispered to everyone,' take a deep breath and let go of what you just saw'.

Everyone looked around at the energy, present in the emerald room, after this vision. Master Shade decided then and there, to clear their thoughts. Suddenly, all the mentors were feeling a little light headed.

Everyone's unique gifts and powers were back on track, like nothing happened, and it all felt balanced and decent. Master Shade then mentioned to Max, "please remove your whiskers from the gold plate, and put them in your satchel".

Max quietly obliged, as he knew other whiskers took the place of the ones he pulled out, immediately. Then, Master Shade shared with everyone present, that there was plenty of things to learn and grow accustom to.

But, overall he and the other Masters were pleased with the outcomes. Then he smiled at the mentors as they knew that they would be able to protect and keep each other comfortable.

Everyone felt connected in that moment once again, as they each knew someone suffered some form of loss. They didn't look at it as loss, but as strength. This assisted the mentors so they could feel encouraged to keep teaching their students.

As for the profound energies that were felt in that emerald room that day, "there were no words". Everyone knew they were family, and Sly recognized that as well. Everyone knew that no matter what happened they were together; connected and transparent.

So they practiced their teachings for the rest of the day and shared thoughts and concerns with Master Shade. On StarDrome all the cells agreed to work without the energy of worry, stress or complaints. That is why the masters have certain places designated for whatever the mentors and students acquire.

All cells agreed to work with positive energy in their blocks, which are considered their community. Next week the mentors will meet the other mentors from Block D.

Block D is in the far North of StarDrome, where the energies are different and there are deep howling winds. The winds are fierce, cold like ice, but the mentors over there don't mind.

The mentors are resilient and carry the energies that will support them through the freezing temperatures of StarDrome. They adapted quite easily, as they have a great Master too! Their Master's name is Stoney Red Water; apparently he comes with the energy of Fire. This master cleanses all the old decay from anything; and works with two flying monkeys named Jonas and Wendy.

All of the mentors in the green room felt fine with meeting the other mentors from Block D, as every cell considers each person as a brother and sister. But it's time, to thank each other, and thank the spirit of energy that you all worked with today, said Master Shade.

'Through your vision and breathing, connect to all parts of your energy system; that you call your skin (body). Come into a relaxed state and thank each other energetically'. Then, we'll meet here next week, at the same time. "Bring your hands to your heart and take a deep breath and give yourselves a hug. Within that moment Master Shade vanished and all the mentors could hear him saying, Thank you." The mentors were glad to go relax…for the evening.

8

The North Side - Block D

Gertrude, Black Cloud and Others

It's been three years and SpiderBoy was tuning in to see where he felt the energy from his dreams. Something bothered him about the energy that he was feeling, and it was to do with Block D. Sly was aware of this block and heard certain things in regards to the other mentors; it didn't feel quite right energetically.

Many of the cell souls landed their pods in different directions, to reside on StarDrome. Sly was in thought with himself as he transcended into a meditative state. He viewed at what was happening in Block D, through his visions.

Sly wasn't sure if the other mentors knew of them, as they were from Block A, but he really wanted to see and clarify a few things. Sly wanted to know what it felt like energetically and what it was like. He already learned from Master Shade not to tune in to things…

Sly knew in that moment he would be protected as SpiderBoy. He shape shifts and proceeds into his visions and turns his energy down to a low key. He first acknowledged the energy of fear, then pulled his energy back into his aura and grounded again. Sly hasn't felt fear since his parents left…

SpiderBoy knew his perceptions were clear and precise. He went into his visions and could actually see Gertrude's energy; she was the first one that emanated into his vision. This didn't surprise him; it felt easier from that point for him to continue remote viewing.

He noticed that Gertrude shape-shifts into a beautiful goddess, and she recognized his energy right away and asked him how he was doing... Sly mentioned to Gertrude, "so what do you call yourself as you shape-shift into this wonderful goddess?"

Gertrude replied, "I am" Surry and SpiderBoy noticed that Gertrude worked with the sun dials and that she could summon night really early. Surry was of Southern Asia descent and apparently her father was of German ancestry, an archeologist... It wouldn't last until her power weakened, he thought; and that all of this was really thought-provoking.

SpiderBoy had to remind himself not to get pulled into the energy, or he would lose himself and leave his body spiritually. He could see that the other mentors were doing a lot of work over there, even as they worked through ice cold temperatures.

SpiderBoy remembers what Master Shade shared about Block D; the temperatures are balanced by all of the mentors working together. One mentor could introduce freezing temperatures and another could bring intense heat...

SpiderBoy then noticed while glancing at Surry. He could see something moving on her left side, it was a striking griffin. This griffin was bathed in clear white, silver, and golden energy, and SpiderBoy was quite surprised because this griffin was bright and clear.

He could be seen from miles away and SpiderBoy recognized that Surry was protected by this griffin. SpiderBoy also saw the beautiful shields Surry had, and he kind of had to look away for a second, and then look again through his third eye.

SpiderBoy was still learning to focus his eyes to see clear visions, sometimes the energy was so brilliant , Sly had to look away until he grew accustom to gazing directly through veils of energy.

SpiderBoy was learning many things from the masters, and this was one of those lessons. Within that moment he was seeing quite clearly into Surry's energy. SpiderBoy decided to see pass certain veils of energy on Surry's right side, because something caught his eye.

He detected a mist of energy, as he was tuning in, and the energy felt familiar to him; it was Black Cloud's energy. "Oh," he says to himself. "Black Cloud can transform his energy into anything he chooses and is from the North Dakota's area...but everyone knows it's written in the Book...

Black Cloud carries a unique sword and it could cut through any rock, if needed." As Sly was focusing on getting a better look, he had to blink a couple times because he felt that the energy within his visions; were becoming brighter.

He cleared the thoughts in his mind with regards to Gertrude's energy, and thanked her for letting him tune in and see how she was doing. And she nodded and asked a similar question telepathically: "How was everyone in Block A?"

Sly mentioned that everyone was fine and he was just being curious about how everyone was doing over there, because he hadn't heard from anyone in a while. A few months have gone by and he didn't hear from Block D. "That's my only reason," he says to Gertrude.

Then SpiderBoy takes a deep breath and he notices Gertrude's energy pull away, and then he closes his eyes and all of a sudden, Jason is right in front of him. Apparently, Sly heard he was from some place called the Ontario region... Jason looks at him from eye to eye, and then within that moment, Jason shape-shifts into a massive black bear, 10 feet tall, at least.

With a body like a tank, Sly had to pull back a few feet because he noticed Black Bear's claws coming out and they looked like steel, and that steel could cut like a knife. Then Sly shrieked, "Whoa! Black Bear, it's me, SpiderBoy, I'm just checking to see how you guys are doing over there in Block D. No disrespect, I'm not coming into your space to upset you or anything." Then Sly pulled his energy back and Black Bear relaxed his...

Black Bear calmed down a bit as he widened his vision, smelled and sensed Spider Boy's energy, he quietly said to him telepathically, "Ok, I will show you what I have been doing."

He shows SpiderBoy with his claws that he can make any incision, if he chooses to; he can infect the (nemesis) with toxins that will harden the blood system. So when those toxins go through the bloodstream, Bear revealed to SpiderBoy that within seconds, any nemesis could be dead.

On the other hand, Black Bear must stay hidden in the eerie part of StarDrome for his powers to last. He wasn't quite sure if he wanted to share that information with SpiderBoy. However, Sly pretended that he didn't hear the last bit of what Jason was thinking, and SpiderBoy knew if Bear came out into light; he had no power.

Therefore, SpiderBoy pretended he didn't hear Bear and thanked him again, for popping in and presenting his energy. At that time he realized that Jason was Judy's brother; and was actually well protected by her.

SpiderBoy grasped he hasn't thought about that for a long time, because he's been too busy taking care of his kids. The other mentors had been busy with Master Shade, and they all had a lot to do.

Black Bear mentioned telepathically to Markus (who is referred to as 'K') that SpiderBoy was investigating and wanted to see how they were all doing. Then all of a sudden Sly felt this great big energy coming in to his space (aura), and Markus stood right beside him, and he abruptly says, "It's ok!', Sly, how are you?" and Sly nodded his head and said, "I'm good, I'm just checking up on you guys, I haven't heard from you in some time."

Markus shakes his head and replies, 'it's great to see you too! Then he smiles and finishes sharing that everyone has been keeping busy, as well. As you know, I'm 'K', and I prefer everyone to call me K', because that aligns my energy with my father.

My father's heritage was very important to me and other members of my family. We have a strong Celtic lineage of men and woman that come from a great blood - line of healers. It does a lot for me in energy, to have the support from my helpers.

I choose not to discuss my father's past, until I'm ready. Besides, everything is kept in the 'Book of Truth' and Master Shade is quite aware of the history. SpiderBoy nods his head and agrees with 'K', that everything sacred stays in the Book.

"OK, I wasn't going to ask you about your dad, said Sly and then he looked straight at 'K' and proceeded to listen to what he had to share; then 'K' mentions to SpiderBoy, that he shape-shifts into Thunderbolts.

Sly noticed Thunderbolt's energy was bright neon pink and blue, with silver edges, Thunderbolts Energy could pierce the ears of all those ones in the night. Sly was just listening for a moment, as 'K' was boasting about himself. K' proceeded to say, that the massive holes he produced with his thunderbolts were at least ten feet deep.

The holes could hold any captive for any amount of time and the nemesis couldn't get out. SpiderBoy noticed that whenever 'K' spoke, it's with precise tones. Every cell knew that 'K' rarely misses; but the caution was 'if 'K' threw too many thunderbolts, he would weaken and would need to rejuvenate with the harvesters.

Sly was just listening and watching through his visions, and realized how many responsibilities each mentor had, including Block D. K' just kept rambling on again, about himself, and K' was in love with Judy.

SpiderBoy was astonished by what 'K' was feeling, because not too many mentors opened up their feelings, the way 'K did. Sly knew Judy was aware of 'K's feelings towards her. She was young and ran away to be with him. When she was only 14 years old; Sly said to K', "Well, didn't that create some difficulties for you there in Block D?"

K shifted his energy and looked at Sly with a peculiar look on his face, and said, "Why would it? She loves me, we're meant to be together, and that's it. No questions asked."

Sly stared at K' and whispered, "Well, don't her parents care?" and K' replied "I'm here to share with you. I don't need any other questions asked. Either you want to hear me or you don't." Sly could feel that 'K was protecting Judy, so he pulled his energy back to give 'K space.

Sly got the hint: "OK, Kai' I'll just listen," everything is written in the 'Book of Truth'. Then K' looked at Sly for a second and said, "Why did you call me Kai?"

"Oh" said SpiderBoy. "I meant K'. My mistake, sometimes my tongue trips over itself."

'K chucked, and he said, "Back to what I was sharing about, Judy. Her parents weren't pleased with her because she ran away to me, but it doesn't matter. Of course they're going to be sad, temporarily speaking, as they still haven't talked to me. But as long as I'm taking care of her, nothing else matters."

My master said it was our choice, as long as we weren't hurting anyone intentionally. Then K' decided to close the conversation telepathically and continue on with his day. He didn't want to discuss anything else and said to Sly, "OK, I'm going to go now. And from now on you can call me Markus, don't even call me K."

Sly gazed at him surprised, and said quietly, "OK, Markus, and thank you for sharing your thoughts with me today. I'm sure others will pop in and let me know how they're doing too." And then K' turned quickly around and his energy moved out of Sly's vision. As soon as he left, Judy came in. She presented herself, as a beautiful eagle.

"Oh," said Sly. "Judy, its SpiderBoy. How are you doing?" She smiled, and came in for a landing. She landed a few feet away from Sly and looked at him, up and down and said, "I'm Eagle Vision.

How are you, SpiderBoy?" Sly replied to Eagle Vision, "We're good, over here in Block A. We're studying and working through a lot of lessons with Master Shade. He keeps us busy with practice and with our students.

"Oh," said Eagle Vision. "Well, Master Winged One is keeping us busy over here, as well. I noticed that you've talked to K." He can't keep anything from me, because we have been together for some time.

"Yes, I did talk to him and he did share that everything is fine, and that you two are together." And she nodded her head and said to Sly, "Well, enough of K'. I'm sure he said plenty. As you know, I helped in the design of StarDrome.

"I didn't know that," alleged Sly. "What a beautiful job, by the way. You are a great designer, a visionary at heart. Very good energy has gone into the design of StarDrome, as I thank the others that you've worked with, also."

"Thank you." Judy felt proud of her self and also mentioned that she had a lot of work to do, as she was always busy. Eagle Vision said she could bring wisdom to the group to share, and support others, in this great time of change.

Sly could sense that Eagle Vision had this deepest depth of precision and could pinpoint any location. She sees everything in red during the day, and blue in the night.

Sly was flabbergasted when Eagle Vision was sharing this with him, as he quietly just listened.

Sly was aware that whenever any of the mentors had anything to share, it was in the Emerald Room, but he wasn't sure what Block D did... as Judy kept sharing everything with him and mentioned her wings protect herself and others.

SpiderBoy realized that Judy was a talker and continued sharing with him, and said," I can protect others also from any of the spheres at night; I was too young when they killed your parents".

SpiderBoy glared through his visions at Judy and said, 'what?' Then she replied,' but I felt sad for you in that moment." And then Sly looked down sadden by what he heard, trying not to go into his emotions, as he was only viewing through his visions.

Then he looked up and whispered, "Its ok, I understand, we were young. Things happen and we move on. I do get regular visits from my parents." Then Judy could sense Sly was hurting from his parents passing.

Judy mentioned to Sly that she was proud of whom she was and we all have amazing teachers, to remind us to stay grounded; so our energies aren't depleted. Then and there she left the conversation telepathically, and they both sensed the quiet and honored their parents in that moment.

Sly had a perplexed expression on his face, from what Judy could see, and she decided to say,' I'm learning quite a bit now, especially in quieting my thoughts.' It has been practice to remind myself to only speak certain things, but I trust you SpiderBoy'. Judy smiled and calmly said, 'I know of you and Luna".

Sly was quite stunned by what Judy said in regards to him and Luna, plus what she shared about quieting the thoughts. He smiled and said," yes, Judy", I'm taking practice too.

Sly then also mentioned with a chuckle,' but we're all telepathic here.' Then he shook his head and thanked Judy for sharing and that he would respect her, by keeping what they shared sacred. It was one of the rules on StarDrome for all the mentors and cell souls to abide by," choice".

Within that moment Judy whispered under her breath, and said, "We're just going to be using our voice."

Then, all of a sudden, Judy hushed what she was saying to Sly, and before she could say another word; Sly shook his head and said calmly,' you don't want to do that.

SpiderBoy glared through his visions strongly and looked at Judy and saw her shaking her head, and hitting herself. Sly could hear her saying out loud,' "There's nothing else that I need to say."

SpiderBoy was shocked by Judy's behavior. He knew it wasn't safe to speak as a human on StarDrome. The masters warned us all, as cell souls to respect the laws of this new world…then he took one last look at Judy and he saw her walk very quickly away.

Then within that instant; Sly could see her shape into Eagle's Vision and fly off. Sly felt that this conversation wasn't over. He didn't quite know what to do with this information and thought he might take this to the next meeting in the green room.

SpiderBoy knew it wasn't in Judy's character not to say goodbye or anything else. But he did notice in her energy as she flew away, one slight thing; he felt the jealousy that oozed through her blood.

Sly closed his visions of Block D and sat there for a second and thought to himself, "Oh my Lord. I'm tuning in quite deeply now and I'm starting to see and sense all of these things with everyone'. I just need to shake this off a little bit." He realized that Judy didn't like anybody looking at Jason either.

Jason was Judy's brother and she protected him and as far as K' is concerned. Judy would kill for him. Sly was disturbed by the energy he felt because he knew that the masters worked hard to keep everything positive and secure on StarDrome. But then he decided to keep this sacred for now and keep an eye out for anything strange in Block D.

Sly recognized within his being, he had to keep some silent power. Sly decided to put this conversation and what he saw in his visions, in his journal, as he knew it was a safe place because no one had the key but him.

He could now feel Judy's energy dissipating as she took off with K'. They went to go finish some kind of task that they had started; from what Sly was sensing intuitively.

Sly was feeling a little depleted, and off in his energy.

He was noticing the energy in his aura and was feeling dissimilar; and he could see the colors in his energy, they looked altered, as well. Within that moment as he was focusing on clearing his space, he heard Angel. She was singing.

Sly adored her beautiful voice and listened, and then Angel said to Sly, "well there you are. I haven't seen you for some time." Sly looked up at Angel quietly, within his peripheral vision, and he noticed the beautiful golden haired beauty, who shone like a million bright lights and could shift into a cougar.

She was called C' for short, everyone just loved her. She believed in balance and fairness. Her one fault was Justice, he was her man and she was only 17 when they got together.

Well, she believed she was 17 years wise. It was her wisdom Justice fell for, not her beauty, and Justice was OK with this. So Angel's gift was to turn anyone to stone who focused on her beauty, anyone who had vanity in their blood.

Sly just silently observed her and listened, because he knew that C' could sense energy from afar, from miles away. She could also perceive who approached in advance.

Sly kept discreet, and he quietly thanked her as he was looking towards his left.

Then Sly said to Angel, 'I'm fine and it is good to see you again; I see that everyone is busy on Block D.' Sly was gentle in his approach because he didn't want to upset Angel, as she was very temperamental.

He quietly thanked Angel for what she shared; He could sense Justice coming. Sly knew that Justice had strong empathic energy because he could sense right away through his energy, that Justice knew he was talking to Angel.

Sly, then realized he needed to shift his energy a little bit and let this conversation go in another direction. Then Justice came in with a great big bang, and then all of a sudden there was a beautiful dragon in front of Sly.

Sly had to step back a little, as he noticed that Justice's body took up a lot of space, he is huge, 20 feet high. Sly could see that Justice had massive wings and he could sense he had an enormous appetite.

Sly understood this dragon could eat everything in sight, he loved everything green, he could eat what he liked and spit out the rest. He wasn't going to keep it because he couldn't digest anything besides greens.

Everyone in Block D called him the veggie king because Justice could eat vegetables, anything green and he can still eat and devour anything in his site. So, the other mentors had to be certain that there was always a plate set aside for him.

Everyone in Block D knew that this dragon could inhabit any terrain, but Justice himself; was forewarned by Master Winged One, not to devour everything in sight; or he would explode. Plus, StarDrome had the season's harvest stored and under a watchful eye, because that harvest needed to be kept to feed the population of cells on StarDrome.

The guardians of the harvest had to be aware that Justice was around, so they created a beautiful place for him to go and stay. But, the only thing was he couldn't take Angel there, this space was made for the dragon energy only.

Justice could consume whatever he needed, in his own space and time. Sly was quite astonished by how much Justice had grown, and then SpiderBoy just heeded, as Justice explained everything to him.

Justice had a good time sharing with SpiderBoy. The energy between them felt good; and they could both feel the love Justice had for Angel. But, Justice had demise, it was Block D.

Sly saw the energy that was running through Justice, which he felt through his heart, as he tuned in. Sly knew that love was there for everyone in Block D, just like Block A. Block D was Justice's family, and because he lost his initial family early, Block D was all Justice knew.

They were all family, it's the only family he has now. Since losing his parents and siblings in the Block raid of the old earth, Justice still has nightmares about it.

These memories are faint, but through Justice's dreams, he sees and hears everything that took place. This is also written in the Book of Truth, and for Justice this is hard on him because he doesn't want to tell anyone.

Sly just listened as Justice shared everything telepathically to him, and then Dragon's Breath remembers it was Angel's family that took him to safety, because Angel told them where Justice was hiding, as she was clairvoyant.

Apparently from what Dragon's Breath said to Sly, Angel could always see into the future. She was taught since an early age. Then Justin said to SpiderBoy,' Thank the universe for my blessings. SpiderBoy nodded and agreed with Dragon's Breath, because he could sense Justice authentically thanks the universe from his heart.

Justice smiled with that precious thought, as he really did swear to protect Angel, no matter what. No questions asked, and Justice was like that, he wasn't going to ask questions, he knew if anyone got in the way, there was a price to pay.

Justice was OK with that because he was already tested, and Sly just listened as Justice continued sharing. Sly said, "Tested? OK, I got a sense that I heard that somewhere before, but I bet you can explain that to me some more."

"Well, I'm going to, said Justice;' you just need to sit and listen." Sly nodded and just paid attention.

Justice shared that he was proud about his test because he already had blood on his hands; and Sly stepped back for a second and just took note. "But it wasn't kept secret. You're probably only the second person I told, said Justice with a frown.

The secret could only be found in the Book of Truth, so I'm not going to share anymore about that. But, my Master Winged One from Block D has the Book. He has everything in that book. All the masters share that Book of Truth…But anyway, apparently, this book holds all fate, all secrets," said Dragon's Breath.

"Oh," said Sly. "I didn't know all of that; as the masters keep everything sacred". Then, Justice whispers and says,' Master Winged One barely speaks of this book, only in an emergency. From what Sly was sensing; Justice was quite sure about that.

SpiderBoy felt that this was too much information for him to indulge in, and pulled his energy back; and put up his boundaries. Then Dragon's Breath said, "Plus, Master Winged One is aware that he didn't want to create another disaster, like the one on the old earth.

Then abruptly Justice turns around, and just about knocks Sly to the ground with his big wing and says,' why did you pull back your energy from me?'. I thought we were friends'.

Then Sly smiles at Justice and states,' we are friends; I just want to make sure no one hears us, that's all. Justice comes in real close to Sly and whispers with his big breath,' I just want this story closed; I don't want you to mention anything to anyone.'

Sly knew instantly, why everyone called Justice, Dragon's Breath,' then he replied back to Justice candidly, fine. 'Anyway, I was here, now I must go look for Angel, I know she was here, I felt her earlier." said Justice, with certainty.

Before Justice left, he said to SpiderBoy, "I remember once overhearing my parents talking to Master Winged One when I was only two." I still recall something being said about the scrolls, the seals were broken on the Book of Truth.'

Justice was certain someone did that purposely, but didn't know who, as he knew that they must be sealed once again. I didn't really understand this conversation because I was a little young. Then Dragon's Breath lifted off the ground and he said to Sly, as he was flying away,' it makes sense with this book, it holds all the vulnerabilities that feed the mind."

Sly couldn't see him anymore, as Justice was gone like the wind. Then Sly just stood there, shook his head and said to him, "Well, I'm not here to talk about all of that, I was just tuning in; to see how you all were doing.

Then, Justice proceeded to tell Sly telepathically from afar, what was happening when Master Winged One spoke to his parents, Anita and Joel. Justice heard clearly as a child that this Book of Truth can be used to harm anyone."

Sly could then sense Justice smiling as he soars high so he could join Angel; and Sly notices that Justice is listening to Angel's voice. All of a sudden, Sly pretended like he wasn't there, he pulled back his energy, and he could hear Angel calling Justice, with this beautiful tone in her voice, "Dragon's Breath! …' Dray…' Dray…"

Sly was stunned, but he still pretended like he didn't notice, because Sly didn't know that Dragon's Breath was called by any other name, but what he knew him as. Sly understood that this was private and noticed that Justice would only let Angel call him that.

No one else, or Justice would pick whoever it was up, and take them to a foreign place. Plus, Sly overheard Dragon's Breath saying to Angel, 'what did you do, this time/'. Just as Sly overheard that, he swallowed hard, as he heard Justice say,' I can't keep covering for you Angel, you're the only girl for me, plus my sister Judy has no hold over us'.

Sly chose to listen, even closer to the conversation, and knew he was running behind to meet up with Master Shade. Sly could hear muffled voices now, and couldn't really make out what Justice was saying to Angel.

But, from what Sly heard, it sounded like this,' Justice said,' there were a few that were listening and that got in the way, he just picked them up; and took them to the barren wasteland.

Sly grabbed his mouth and he swallowed hard, and he was shocked by what Justice just said, because he heard of this barren wasteland, from the masters. Sly realizes he must quit tuning in, to everyone's business.

The parents shared of this place, before they died, that no one was supposed to go to the barren wastelands. The masters called those places the dry lands, and Sly just listened and he heard Justice say that there is no water in these dry lands, there's only rock.

"Hmm," Justice just kept thinking. And at the same time, Sly just heard this all telepathically, as Justice was sharing with Angel. Through his visions, Sly could see both of them clearly. This time he wasn't trying to hear or see, but realized as SpiderBoy, his senses were stronger.

He saw Angel as she was standing by a unique tree, because Sly knew this tree didn't grow where he was housed. This tree could play tricks on the mind of the person standing beside it, especially if they weren't aware of its potential powers.

Then Sly remembers back to the teachings Master Shade was sharing, and he called the tree,' Coyote Stands. Master Shade also said, it could transform itself into a small boy, to trick you into helping him; then he has you under his spell…and Coyote even has locked some spirits in the tree.

Sly, then had to remind himself, to pull his thoughts back and keep focused on where he was, so he wouldn't get pulled back through time.

Sly glanced up to see Angel shape into a cougar, with open arms to greet Justice. She seemed so small compared to Dragon's Breath. Angel was beautiful, and Sly could see how they made a good pair, just like him and Luna.

Then Sly shook his head a couple times and he realized that he should let Angel and Justice go, so he could meet up with Master Shade. But, before he closed his communications, he heard Justice say, "Angel doesn't need to know this, Sly.

'Angel doesn't need to know that I take these souls to the barren wastelands. Because she would be devastated, it's important that it stays quiet." Sly heard what Dragon's Breath said precisely, loud and clear; and said "Ok, Ok, Justice, I didn't hear anything at all."

Within that moment, Justice knew that Sly was going to keep quiet or else…

Sly just said, "I will see you guys. I'm out of here."

That's when Justice met up with Angel, and they went off to enjoy their day, as it was important because if Angel ever found out, Justice would be very distraught.

It wouldn't just be Justice that would be upset; it would be Angel who would be very disappointed as well, at Justice, because she looks up to him, as her angel.

Justice looks at Angel, as his angel. So there would be some very upsetting energy in both Blocks, and Sly felt saddened to be threatened. Justice wants it kept as a secret in the Book of Truth.

Sly just took a deep breath and he shook himself free from that energy and he didn't want to be connected to it anymore. Because he didn't want to be seen or have anyone feel that energy from Block D, or from the Book of Truth.

Especially, Master Shade, because he would know they were doing something that they're not supposed to be doing. As they're still mentors, still learning, and it was important for all of us; as mentors to do the right thing.

Sly was thinking, that StarDrome and the planetary systems had universal laws that they promised to live by, while inhabiting StarDrome. The laws keep the balance and the energy agreeable for all planetary systems.

Sly realized within that moment, through that meditative state, that there are things that he can't share with others, because they have their own Book of Truth. Their Masters hold their secrets, as well. Consequently; each different block has a different book and key, so Sly didn't know what to do with that information.

SpiderBoy knew he wanted to proceed with his visions, to see who else was going to show themselves from Block D, so he decided to tune in to Master Shade and let him know he was going to be late. Suddenly, Master Shade was checking up on him telepathically and energetically.

Master Shade mentioned to SpiderBoy, 'mind your own business', and Sly knew he heard this phrase before. Then he said to Master Shade,' I'm learning a lot today,' see you shortly. Sly could then sense Master Shade pulling his energy out of his aura.

Sly was preparing to see who else was in his visions, as he finished sharing with Master Shade. He noticed Andrew shaping into Wind Walks. His energy grows massively strong, through gusts of wind, each time he gets angry or frustrated with anything.

Wind Walks leaves nothing but the twigs on the trees, and Sly documented this and saw how fast Andrew grew and he recognized within his being, that Andrew's energy could release up to 300 miles of wind. There was nowhere to hide on StarDrome because she was wide open and free.

Sly realized that Wind Walks could destroy anything on StarDrome, even the massive Sour Figs, which Block D called the Old Ones. These Sour Figs were the antennas for

StarDrome, so the Old Ancients could call the old world. Wind Walks was left cleaning up the mess he made, when practicing his shifts. Then he would casually say,' oh, well, that was accidental, it just blew away by it, and then he would shrug his shoulders and laugh.

But with everybody in Block D, they just knew it was one of those hard lessons that Wind Walks was going to learn. Or else the masters would have him cleaning up more... and he just kept things to himself, this way he wouldn't be answering to Master Winged One; so he thought.

All of a sudden, Sly detected something, as Andrew was showing him these telepathic pictures through his visions. Wind Walks was really upset one time and accidentally propelled special things into this secret corner, where the tides meet on StarDrome.

Sly was shocked again because it seemed like Block D was becoming imbalanced, then he just listened to Andrew; as he shared with him. Suddenly, Wind Walks showed Sly that he could be very disruptive with his energy, his flow, and then he instantly created a disruption with the water beings.

SpiderBoy had to immediately come to rescue his dear friends, the water beings once again. He reminded Wind Walks to keep balance with the water because it takes a long time for the water to flow, undisturbed. Then Wind Walks sent all his angry winds, into that secret corner.

This way he could protect StarDrome from any pain, as she was an empathic planet. But, Wind Walks explained to SpiderBoy, that he couldn't contain the winds there, unless he was calmed down. The only thing that could calm him was the black root from the Licorice Tree.

This tree only grew on the highest ridge of StarDrome, in the East, but it was protected by outlaws; which were the scavengers left over from StarDrome's first war. She promised them, they could stay only if they protected this rare tree.

If anyone was to pick from her, this black root, the scavengers would want a fair trade. It was your teeth; they liked to chew on teeth. Master Golden Ear was the only one with magic, to create such teeth.

It was in the precise mixing of ingredients, or else the outlaws would know instinctively that they weren't the real teeth. In any case the outlaws would take what they wanted, and that meant anything, so the exchange must be made by the same token.

Within that moment Sly took a deep breath, and sighed and saw the mental pictures of the flood created by Wind Walks himself. The disruption to the water beings was horrendous and there had to be a lot of healing done with the water. Sly knew very well, that all is sacred on StarDrome.

There was a flood in Block D and Wind Walks had a lot of explaining to do with his Master, about his power and what he was learning. There were no more excuses, because he learned many times, and he was 23 years wise.

The other mentors knew he had a way with the masters that he could balance things, and it seemed to be that Wind Walks wanted some kind of control, just to prove he was almighty.

Apparently, Master Winged One had taken Wind Walks into several different practices and the lessons to teach Andrew how to set balance with the elementals. There was also someone else from Block D, who had to learn how to set precedents in regards to balance.

Block D had to help clean this mess up that Wind Walks made, because if one got into mischief the others had to learn from the mischief, as they would teach each other, and learn from each other, as a group family..

Things would shift positively and this was a powerful lesson that Master Winged One liked to teach without delay. This gave Winged One some needed rest, so he could plan his visits to the other blocks on StarDrome with the other Masters.

SpiderBoy recognized that Wind Walks was sort of a loner, he just didn't want anyone around him and he felt misunderstood. He had a secret love, it was Mazie. Sly was quite surprised by that, because Mazie's from Bock A, and then he felt the energy in his heart chakra.

When he tuned into Andrew, Sly realized how much Mazie was missed by him. What Sly heard next from Wind Walks was, that it was his secret; and it is written in the Book of Truth.

Andrew felt guilty, because he was from Block D and Mazie was from Block A, they were separated and weren't supposed to be together, because of all this nonsense. Different mentors with unique gifts to teach the other cell souls, on their Block.

But Master Winged One didn't know that Andrew really cared for Mazie, and the funny thing, was Mazie cared for Andrew, too. SpiderBoy didn't realize that Andrew's heart was broken, because he was from Block D. He was chosen to be one of the mentors there.

Sly felt Andrew's energy through his heart chakra and recognized what it felt like, to miss someone so deeply. SpiderBoy knew he would feel similar to Andrew, if he missed Luna too.

Then Andrew understood within that moment what Sly declared as love with Luna. Andrew had mentioned to Sly that there wasn't any other love for him, but Mazie, 'no one' but Mazie.

Sly just nodded his head and telepathically said to Andrew, "I understand. I feel the same way about Luna, but we must keep it quiet." Then Andrew quietly left and shared that he wanted to spend time by himself. Sly just thought for a moment, "Maybe I'm visiting too long

I'll just check out one more mentor, through my visions.

I'm not really doing any harm, Sly thought to himself; I'm just checking up on them. Plus, I will need to shake this energy off right now. Luna's going to sense all this energy from the mentors.

Sly also felt that Andrew will be OK, and however the masters' decide to teach, they'll assist in harmonizing the energy again." Sly was still quite surprised because Mazie's energy didn't reveal anything in regards to Andrew, not at all, she must be really good at hiding things, Sly thought to himself.

Sly was quiet within that moment he realized that someone was standing on his right side. He gave himself a shake again and he took a deep full breath, "Oh."

He quietly said to Sage, "It's you." "Yes it's me," said Sage. "How are you? You don't come to visit very often."

"Well," said Sly. "I've been busy, and I see that you've been busy over here in Block D.

We haven't heard from all of you in probably a few months now."

Sage nodded and she shape-shifted into a beautiful medicine keeper. She carried the Book of Spells from every single incarnation, it was a big book. She was from Romani origin as her father came from a simple line of people from Anatolia…Sly was quite surprised that Sage could handle her responsibility, but he knew that was her gift, and no one else had that book but her.

Sly was very cautious with his difference of opinion, because if any person is holding on to the Book of Spells; you would chose to be careful with your words. So he smiled at Sage while she shared, and he was mesmerized by her beauty.

Sage had the biggest smile that had the deepest color of red; like a cherry, her hair was black like coal, her skin was cool to the touch. Sage didn't like to be seen much or heard. She chose to keep distant.

Sage chose her time wisely with the masters; she would break out in hives or rashes, if she got too close to heat, or the sun. Sly remembered that a little bit, 'Oh! He quietly said to himself, so he won't remember because he was there, when it happened, so long ago.

Sage mentions to SpiderBoy, "Listen to me now. I'm sharing something with you that I haven't shared for a long time."

Sly said, "Ok." Then Sage glanced at him and she said, "I had these scans done on me, energetically before, to prove things." Sage told Sly she has memories of when she was turning 13, " I do remember, she says to Sly, "but I don't want to remember."

Sly nodded his head, and he said telepathically, "I do, too."

Then Sage said repeatedly to Sly, "Listen, I'm going to share this with you now. I need to say what I am feeling. I get tired of guys, because they don't listen to me." Sly understood what she was saying, he is aware, she was holding the Book of Spells!

Sly just nodded his head, so Sage could proceed and finish what she had to share. Then Sage abruptly said, "Markus was playing a joke on me. He wasn't really thinking it was a joke and he didn't think that it was going to hurt me." Sly could see tears in her eyes as she shared.

Sage felt everything as she was a strong empath and was considered too sensitive by her peers. Sly understood, as he was also a disciplined empath as well. Sage said that "K got out of hand, out of order with his disrespectful thoughts."

Gertrude couldn't come to aid her at that time, either, as it probably would have caused pain or danger emotionally Sage remembers her old friend Lance. Sly hasn't heard from Lance for a long time, and he really doesn't know where Lance is.

Thinking about it, Sly had that thought for a second while Sage was still sharing with him; then Sage continued to say to Sly, "Lance came to my rescue, he put out the fire that Justice created, and lifted me out of that hole, and proceeded to fill those holes with water."

Sly just listened, and remembered some of the pieces of that puzzle, and then all of a sudden, Sage utters, "K would make those holes in the ground with his thunderbolts, and they were very deep, as you know, they're more than ten feet deep."

It wasn't funny, because Sage was being dragged and placed into a hole, and told that she's meant to stay there, like the child you are. "Think about it, if you're thirteen, and these are supposed to be your friends, and they put you in a hole? Hmm, this wasn't a good sign," said Sage.

Sage cries, "I still have a scar. Do you remember that, Sly?" Sly looked around and slowly said, "Yeah."

"Well, from your answer," said Sage, "I'm pretty sure you don't remember, I'm disfigured, and this scar on my back doesn't go away.

This scar has healed and it has a thick mark in a circle, on my back, and within that circle, there are other circles. They're thick disgusting scars and sometimes still tender to touch."

Sage kept resilient with memories of her grandmother, who passed when she was five, and Sage's grandmother taught her about the herbs and the medicine, at that time.

Sage reminded Sly that she was taught many things from her grandmother, and because of those teachings she was able to put medicine on her burns. She told Sly, she thanks her grandmother every day.

Sly just listened to Sage and he knew that she just needed to share her feelings because it had been a long time since this incident happened with 'K. Sly realized why he was tuning in to Block D and figured he would just listen to what they had to say.

Sage mentioned to Sly that she was very grateful for everything she grew to understand about herbs and roots. Sage was able to make a special poultice to put on her burn on her back,

The healing occurred, but Sly felt that Sage has a hard time to walk away from what happened; even though 'K apologized. She still remains angry about it, especially being housed in Block D where 'K resides too.

The masters reminded Sage of the importance of forgiveness and taking these concerns to circle to share amongst the other mentors. But, she still gets to see everybody that played that joke on her and she knows that she'll be able to forgive it one day, but not now.

Then she gazes up at Sly and thanks him for listening, and then states, "I have to go, I have my young ones to teach, and it was nice seeing you again, Sly."

Then she quietly said, "I'll work on forgiveness, but Markus is one of those guys that has a behavior that is hard to forgive."

She just walked away from Sly's vision and he just nodded and he said, "Ok. It was nice talking to you, Sage, I'll see you again." Sly couldn't feel anything else in the energy, it was getting nice and cool now, and the temperatures were dying down.

Sly realized he was shifting back into this neutral place, in his body. He was happy by what he just experienced from some of the mentors, from Block D. Sly had to question himself in regards to all the things shared with him. Everything was meant to be shared in private, but sometimes as mentors we just need to lend an ear...

He senses now that he probably has to visit Block D, a little more regularly and maybe mention to Block D; that they should visit Block A and get together in the Emerald Room. Sly knew he was inquisitive, but he was tuning in because he was curious and wanted to hear positive things etc.

Sly believed he could choose to check out some of the other blocks, on StarDrome; but he knows the masters are doing that already. It wasn't Sly's responsibility and the masters don't mention anything private, to any of us mentors. So, Sly knew that it was a terrible idea but he couldn't resist.

Within that moment Sly was already thinking about tomorrow, as he wants to check up on Tanis and Gordon and the rest of the mentors from Block D, without master Shade knowing. He felt good with all the things shared, as he knew he would keep quiet, because these things were sacred between all mentors.

This way the information can't be used to hurt anyone today or any other time on StarDrome. He takes a deep breath and realizes his vision is getting stronger through his senses. He was quite astonished, and he knows that he's going to keep some of this quiet; he's not going to share it with Master Shade yet.

Sly decided to see if Master Shade and Master Winged One can bring this information together, to assist their mentors. Sly was aware there was a lot of information coming from all the mentors, from the different blocks on StarDrome. The Masters had a lot of work ahead of them, and he admired that.

Sly just said OK to his grandfathers and grandmothers, telepathically, as he was told by them; he was getting too involved with the other mentors difficulties...' I'm just going to leave this one alone', he sent a telepathic message out to his mother because he missed her dearly.

Sly said out loud to his mother,' if there's anything that you'd like to add, in regards to Block D, just let me know'. 'Is there anything that I need to be cautious about? 'Just let me know! Sly sent love and hugs to his mom and dad and to all the other souls that were out there in that realm of existence; after death.

He acknowledged in that moment, that any soul passed, could choose to visit him and the rest of the mentors, especially if any of the mentors had questions to ask them at any time. But right now Sly felt satisfied with what he had accomplished in his meditation, and he realizes now that he must go and do some work with Master Shade.

Until we meet again.

9

Disappearances

Suspicions Linger

Gordon is also one of the mentors from Block D and he shape shifts into Termite Hills, a swift moving energy of speed and agility. He can build mountains of dirt and rock anywhere he chooses on StarDrome.

He can devour anything in sight, as Gordon's command of energy pathways are strengthening through his telekinesis placement. Gordon's only weakness in placement of energy is the mighty torrential rains of mentor Augustine.

Gordon hasn't seen Augustine or Wind Walks since they were carried to the barren lands by Justice. Termite Hills realized that he missed them; as they all worked well together and had amazing gifts. Gordon believes and knows that the great Winged One taught them well.

With this thought Gordon smiled as he remembered the time when Augustine was battling for his love, Angel. Well, so he thought at that time, but as everyone knows in Block D; Justice sees to all of that.

When it comes to his lady love Angel, Justice makes sure no one is getting to close or upsets Angel. He didn't like it when Angel was upset because she threatened to leave him.

Gordon believes that Augustine will one day; seek revenge on Justice with the others that were re - located to the barren lands. The masters referred to the barren lands, as the Bad Lands.

Gordon for now, kept his thoughts secure and quiet, but as for Termite Hills, he stayed in disagreement and open telepathically to any sign of discord, until he heard of Amanda.

She was from Block B. He only heard of her by mistake, but it was destined for Gordon to overhear the masters describe Amanda's talents just as he was entering the healing room.

Gordon believes and knows intuitively that he wants to be transferred to Block B, so that he can be with Amanda. His heart was being pulled intensely by Amanda's energy; the only way Gordon can be transferred is by passing his tests.   Gordon already had several tries with the masters, but they didn't make it easy for him because they wanted him to be certain of what he was sensing.

For the mentors it was their way of keeping the mentors on track, he said to himself. It was crucial for mentors to be aware, as they grew. Through thought Justice takes Gordon deeper into his unique abilities, through meditation. Amanda can hear his cry for love and peace, so that they can be together.

Gordon knew one thing, that Justice uses his power without thinking, he just does. Can you imagine taking Augustine to the barren lands? Gordon understood he had to be on Justice's good side and keep his thoughts to himself regarding his friends.

Somehow Gordon knew he would figure out a way to help the other mentors escape the Bad Lands. He would always remember Augustine as a mentor, to him. He has the gift of the torrential rains to create downpours and to somehow escape.

In that moment, Termite Hills realized through his visions, it must be the wetlands now. Gordon remembers when Augustine shared with him that his parents were from this beautiful place called Hawaii…Then he smiled to himself and thought for sure Augustine was creating something of use. Gordon then chose to quiet his thoughts, to take a deeper look into his visions.

He could see where Augustine and the rest of the mentors were, in the Bad Lands. Gordon already knew he and others were warned not to look too deep, otherwise; you can put yourself into that dimension.

Especially if you're working with your vision, it takes a lot of practice not to get involved. Gordon eased his energy, and out of curiosity, he let his intentions go deeper into his screen to have a better look.

To his amazement, he found himself on top of a large protruding rock, a big rock cliff. Gordon walked towards his right side and looked down into the valley below. To his surprise, he saw a stream of water, cascading down from a mountain, and it was surrounded by lush greens, reds and blues.

From the corner of his left eye; he saw a flash of light, and all of a sudden he saw a massive dragon was landing by his right side. This dragon was coming in fast and startled him, back into his body from his depth of vision.

Gordon immediately opened his eyes from his visions, and said out loud, "That must be 'Roth. He is so big and powerful!' He grew so much, since Justice put him in the Bad Lands." We all heard this story; Roth was only 10 years wise, when Angel demanded he disappear…

Gordon could hear Roth scream angrily, "Get Justice to get us out of here or you'll see damage like you've never seen obliteration before."

Gordon had to immediately grab his ears, as the high vibration of the Dragon's Breath, made his ears go weak, momentarily. That was all Termite Hills needed to hear, so he would stop investigating what happened to the mentors in the Bad Lands...

He just shook his head and body, so he didn't hear and see his visions of the Bad Lands. Gordon preferred to tune into Amanda and her energy in Block B. Gordon picked up his rake and went outside to help in the gardens. He knew he needed to shake this memory of what he heard there were many gardens to work within, to keep busy.

Gordon started whistling and left the healing room behind in his thoughts. But, he was concerned by Roth's anger towards Justice and Angel, as the masters didn't know who raised him.

The Bad Lands is a space in the far South of StarDrome where nothing grows, as far as the masters knew. Nothing but deep caves and rocks, the dust storms were horrendous, anyone caught in the storms could be smothered and easily choked to death.

It wasn't a pleasant emotion for Justice to carry anyone off to the Bad Lands. He didn't realize the consequences of his actions in detail. All he knew was he was abiding to Angels' wishes by getting rid of anyone that posed a problem to his beloved girlfriend.

The masters made sure that Justice set some kind of balance through karmic law, for what he had done numerous times; by placing mentors in the Bad Lands. The masters knew that Justice took the mentors from other blocks (districts) to the Bad Lands.

As a karmic pay back, Justice was kept away from Angel for a few months, until the energy was repaid. What the masters didn't know; was Justice and Angel devised a plan to get even, one day, so that no one kept them apart. 'No,' One.

Roth's name is Dragon's Breath, and shape-shifts into a Dragon. His main gift; was his breath, called the 'Fire of Hell. Where the echoes are heard repeatedly across the lands, the echoes were the energies of all the souls that Dragon's Breath consumed.

It was Roth's mission to clear the karma, and eventually release the souls he kept locked away for centuries. It was time to let them out, so they could start anew on StarDrome and other planetary systems.

Roth was aware of this vision since birth, as he always had to work with letting go of anger before it turned into rage. The energy of rage consumed its victims; no one knew it was written in the 'Book of Truth'.

Only, Master Winged One, and the other masters, knew what had happened when Roth was only two years old. The young Roth grew so angry at his parents, he couldn't' stop his rage and it consumed both his parents instantly.

He found both their bracelets on the floor, once he cooled down. He took off for a few days until the masters found him in a treetop, they never asked him how he got there, and never mentioned this episode again.

The masters all knew that one day it would come out, as Roth needed to heal his wounds. To heal from that wound the most, but forgiveness was the key, but first to himself. No one knew but Roth, that he repeatedly remembered seeing the fire consume his parents. But he didn't realize that it was him in the practice.

Roth still carries his parents' bracelets to remind him of his their fate. Those bracelets are kept near his heart now, as he inquired about the spell that was needed to shrink those bracelets. This way he could keep them close to his heart.

It was because of his dear friend Sage. Roth knew that he owed her a favor, for silence, because no spells were to be used until they were older. Because when they were younger they were naïve and still learning. Plus the masters always warned the mentors, that spells were dangerous until we understood.

So those secrets are kept in the Book of Truth, also. There are many things for the mentors to accomplish, as the masters are learning many things from the ancient ones, the ones that came before them.

Many parents have visited their children on different blocks, through apparitions and some through dreams. They were reminding the children of things yet to come on StarDrome. Luna's mother came to visit her in a vision and reminded her that she had some powerful gifts, taking place as she shape-shifted into Swift One.

Luna awoke and she was surprised by the sight of these wings that her mother showed her in her dreams. She couldn't really remember the vision because her mother said it wasn't time.

She also reminded Luna that it was something special she would share with her future husband. Luna kept this secret quiet, as she didn't want to bring it to anybody's attention, because she was concerned that someone won't understand what her mother was sharing.

She decided to sit with Master Shade for a little while, and he explained to her that it was part of her process, as she was shape-shifting. It was something sacred from a mother to her daughter and it was Luna's message to figure out.

Master Shade meditated with Luna to assist her in obtaining the rest of her message, as master helped Luna go deep into trance. Master Shade could see Luna smiling and tears were flowing from her eyes.

Master felt the intense energy of the message being received through Luna's vision because he could sense Luna had flight, when the time came. Luna shared with Master Shade what she saw, 'I become a very beautiful Pegasus and I still carry the gifts of speed, strength and agility.

Master watched in vision as Luna shared with him, he could see her movements were graceful at the same time, as she moved with ease. She also mentioned to Master Shade that this had to be 'private' until she married; he then nodded and assured Luna that all was kept safe with him.

Luna never mentioned this sacred knowing to SpiderBoy. He still doesn't know to this day. One day Luna wants to surprise SpiderBoy with her gift of flight. But, right now SpiderBoy is learning how to ride and hang on tight for dear life; as she almost takes flight through the exercises.

SpiderBoy shares his concerns with Luna, that she is too fast for a spider, then he chuckles and he tries to hang on to her mane. Luna is aware that SpiderBoy is practicing using his webs.

SpiderBoy smiles at Luna and replies,' wait until I'm on your back again, flying through the air. Luna was seeing those visions clearly once again and she giggled at SpiderBoy and said shyly,' you're so cute Sly. Then he grinned and whispered to Luna, 'I will be okay, you'll see.

The night is coming so it's time for the mentors to close things down so others can rest, and the guardians can keep watch on StarDrome. This is a good time when it's quiet, it's sacred.

Some cells decide to go into their dreams and others may choose to meditate before they rest. They usually receive many messages either way from the universe and loved ones.

There's lots of energy work being done at night. The masters are busy watching and taking care of the writing that they need to put it in the books. Without the masters busily at work, it would be despair to anyone on StarDrome. The masters come together tomorrow to share their talents and their gifts with each other.

The masters make sure that everything is functioning positively in the other blocks, and then they check on the mentors. To make sure that their students are learning, understanding and sensing the very things taught to them daily. Resulting in experiences that last a life time as StarDrome is Healing…

10

Book of Truth

What's in the book?

Kira and Louise were also taken to the Badlands by Justice. This was all done by Angel's request, as Angel had her own protective way that worked with her jealousy towards others. Angel got what she wanted: for no other woman to look at Justice, ever. Louise was Angel's best friend from childhood when they were residing on old earth

When they first arrived at StarDrome the girls were transferred to Block C, with other cell souls. Once they grew in their abilities, the masters knew where to relocate them. Both girls were split up.

Angel was directed to Block D, and Louise was taken to Block F. These transfers were reliant on each soul's gift and the teachings that needed to take place. This is how the masters knew weaknesses over strengths with each mentor.

The masters always mentioned in their teachings that the weaknesses needed to become strengths or the energy would eventually deteriorate someone through their gifts, if not reinforced with positive intention.

The energy of weakness plays a role, mentally, emotionally and physically in each cell that is still healing and learning many things. Balance is the key, especially through all human-like aspects. Each soul who chooses to be transported to the new world knows that behavior had to change.

Thoughts had to be calmed and choices had to be made to open one's energy for the new world. The parents of each gifted child knew since their arrival to StarDrome, that they would perish. They knew that their energies couldn't match the high frequencies on StarDrome, after leaving old earth.

But the masters agreed with the parents that no child would know of these circumstances because it would create some turmoil on StarDrome. The masters didn't allow lower frequency energies, none whatsoever.

The masters taught the mentors because they were chosen to teach the younger children, through each masters' knowledge. This way all new energies were strengthened to grow, harvest and live the new life on StarDrome.

All the young souls who are now in the care of each mentor has little knowledge of what their parents agreed to, by taking them to a new world. Everything is still secretly kept and written in the Book of Truth. The Book of Truth is huge and has the colors of black and gold.

There is only one golden key to unlock this Book and no one but Master Winged One knows where the key is kept. Many words of wisdom are written in the great book and each master carries a unique key to unlock their section, as it is named alphabetically.

Many mysteries have been written and locked in the Book of Truth, secrets of the old earth's demise and struggles. The suffering that was caused by the people through each other's disrespect was ruthless.

The chosen ones for the new world and the sacrifices that were made are also kept in the Book, the creation of the pods. The delicate energies of all those amazing teachers who chose to stay behind and die. All these things are written and cataloged in the Book of Truth.

It is imperative for the Book of Truth to be protected, so no one could use what was written to harm that person... It was agreed by each cell, to start a new life destined for some other planet in the galaxy. That is how StarDrome came to be the choice for many of the cells leaving old earth.

The Book of Truth is sacred and is the responsibility of all the masters on StarDrome, to keep it that way. Kira was 18 years old, well wise and she was called the Harvester, the one who can reap and give so much back to the earth.

She shared her harvest with all the blocks on StarDrome that were communities, through what she grew. Her energy could pass healing deep into the StarDrome's crust and things would immediately start to blossom, where something could not grow previously.

Where there was dead energy, now there was new growth. The colors and the depth of the new harvest were astonishing. Kira always knew the accurate times to plant, she also knew the seasons of StarDrome well. It took a lot of time for Kira to receive the visions through meditation, to get the energy just right for planting and harvesting.

The crops do not grow well without Kira's support. She taught only a few cells about her medicines. Some of them are harvesting and planting new things on StarDrome, but the intensity of energy is lacking. The masters and mentors support each other as much as they can, but now she's in the Badlands.

She can probably create new growth and harvest there, but the other mentors on StarDrome miss her energy and giggles around them. The little ones she was teaching miss her deeply as well; Kira was mentoring two little girls, twins, when she was taken by Justice, to the Badlands.

The two young twins cried profusely and weren't strong enough emotionally and mentally yet, they were only six years wise. The masters chose to transfer them to the Island of Misfits, as it was the place destined for souls that were slow moving and needed more time to re-adjust.

The cells that were transferred to the Island lost their faith, in their abilities and teachings. This was seen as a weakness to the masters because all the mentors had to be well balanced and taught correctly by the ancients.

The energy of weakness couldn't be seen or felt on StarDrome, as it would lessen the energy of protection and create war. The masters agreed through universal law that they would remain silent, when it came to making any remarks, demands or decisions about the island.

Anything about the Island was kept secret, the only thing heard was the name of the Ancient that resided there and taught the children. His name was César. He was destined to take care of the Island when he was young by his father and generations before him.

Not too many cells heard about the Island and didn't dare ask or inquire about the children that were placed there. One could visit once, if they chose to share the energy of joy and happiness, but no sadness of any kind was welcomed on the Island.

The Island and its inhabitants are kept private and are written in the Book of Truth as well.

11

Angel and Louise

Negative Intentions

Louise was still saddened by all the things that had transpired since her and Angel grew apart. Louise chose to send good energy to Angel all the time, and to those cells that needed it. Louise promised to watch over Angel. Angel really promised to watch over Louise and not let anything get in the way of their friendship.

Until, Angel met Justice of course. Angel was love-struck by Justice and Louise tried to confide in her about Justice and his behavior. Justice shared some words quietly to Louise and others about his feelings towards Angel.

But, Master Winged One said that all mutterings were to be shared in the Green Room. It was one of the laws agreed by the masters for StarDrome, to keep the sacredness between each cell soul private. If anything needed to be shared, it could either be shared there or in the healing room, on each block.

As mentors we all knew that the masters mentioned the Book of Truth and other important messages regularly on different occasions. Louise was 21 years wise and loved life and wanted to create everything new and green, as long as it was providing a service to others on StarDrome. Louise was thrilled with the outcomes she had made on StarDrome, and now in the Badlands.

Louise and Augustine created the best damn place to live, with others. With hard work and dedication everyone who participated in the creation of transforming the wastelands was stoked. Louise remembers back to when they had first arrived in the Badlands, it was hot, dry, dusty, and there was this smell of sulfur in the air.

That sulfur made all their noses bleed except for Roth, of course, because he was fire. Roth was the sacred breath. Thank goodness that all of the mentors placed in the Badlands together got along and chose to help each other. But it was Louise's concern with the other mentors from block D that Roth is out to seek some sort of revenge with; not just on Justice but all of StarDrome.

Roth believed that no one cared because no one came to rescue them from the wastelands. Lincoln was close to Louise since they first met in Block C. Lincoln was called the Seed Carrier, as he had the gift to plant the most sacred seeds of all.

When the seeds were placed in Lincoln's right hand, his energy would emanate a beautiful silver light around the seeds. Then within a flash there was this wonderful bright light that invigorated the seeds so that they would be ready for planting.

Lincoln always had the gift for planting, so he always played in the soil or sand when he was young on the old earth, when it was still habitable. Kira was his adopted sister, but no one knew…

Being 20 years wise now, he knew that the seeds he brought with him from the old earth can't be seen or used. Lincoln didn't know if he could grow them there in the new world, because he already noticed the frequency of energy was changing the color of the old seeds.

They went from the iridescent color of gold to purple. They were once light brown. Lincoln was sure the seeds were becoming miracle seeds. He had visions of what these seeds could do. The only weakness that Lincoln felt was the secrecy to plant these seeds and keep anyone from finding out.

Lincoln realized in that moment how much his earth seeds needed to be nurtured and watered, as Lincoln could hear them moaning for the land. He tried desperately to keep them quiet so no one else could hear their cries. The only setback is water, as StarDrome placed restrictions on the consumptions.

All the water in StarDrome is being handed out and given to each Block differently. Only the mentors that worked with the water beings could request anything from them, and Lincoln knew from previous interactions that Sly wasn't going to take on any burdens relating to this task.

Lincoln and Sly knew the masters' warning about taking extra water for anything. The teachers knew that once something was changed energetically, the energy was different. There wasn't any waste, as everything was crucial to survival, the masters vowed to live a life full of promise especially after what happened on old earth.

Lincoln always knew that Louise worked with gold dust as she was always connected to the Fairy Kingdoms. The fairies would only come out and make themselves known to real truth, to the ones that spoke wisdom.

Louise always took Lincoln to the Fairy Kingdoms. This was kept quiet between them, but the masters knew. Well, Master Silver Tooth would have separated them for sure because only certain mentors were permitted to work or be in the Fairy Kingdoms to protect them.

It was hard enough; they both missed each other dearly, even now since Louise was carried off by Justice. Louise keeps quiet about it, but can sense Lincoln tuning in and wanting to help her somehow. She wants to go slow with Lincoln because she doesn't want Justice or Angel getting disappointed with him.

Sometimes Louise feels rushed or manipulated into working with Lincoln so they can find a way back to the other Side of StarDrome. Louise is quite empathic to the needs of others including watching over Lincoln. He must respect her wishes and work harder to prove himself to Louise and her family in the Bad Lands.

Lincoln was respected by Louise's parents' and best friends. He always disliked her parents and he didn't trust them completely. Louise's father dictated to her how she was to live and he tried to make her choices for her...with some luck he succeeded.

He couldn't stop Louise from coming to StarDrome to keep her protected, well, also to keep her on track. There was so much more to that part of Louise's life and Lincoln believed that it was written in the Book of Truth.

No one really knew what anyone went through before StarDrome...or about Lincoln's past; it's just that the masters keep everything quiet and sacred. It's the law of the universe or else the masters could sense any energy out of place, out of rhythm.

When the pattern of energy on StarDrome is out of order, she doesn't run smooth. StarDrome's energy is becoming stronger with each passing day as long as the mentors keep teaching and growing a new race of Star Seeds.... One day the mentors quietly plan to visit the Island and take the children home with them, but they must confirm this intention with the Old Ancient...but for now they will consider creating peace and harmony between all Blocks on StarDrome.

12

The Energy of StarDrome

Energy Vibration

StarDrome is becoming a very stunning place, the energy is high and the frequencies are very balanced, as all of the mentors are becoming enlightened. They are quite empathic in their energies especially when working with their students.

The younger children have grown as well and are becoming uniquely disciplined in their art or skills. The mentors have done exceptionally decent work. Each day the classes are growing and hold up to 24 children for each mentor.

Many different children are coming from dissimilar planetary systems to learn and work with their unique abilities. Out of those 24 children you have two mentors teaching continuous lessons that seem endless. Master Shade and others prefer that lessons are taught this way.

This discipline shows that StarDrome is methodical and organized. The twelve masters work hard teaching what they know to their mentors, who were chosen from birth. The masters left the old earth, before it suffered its destruction. The masters prepared the energy on StarDrome.

To assure everything was in alignment for when the other families came in their pods to make StarDrome their new home. This action and discipline to prepare for StarDrome wasn't easy, even for the masters. Everything is written and will continue to be written in the Book of Truth.

This exercise for departure of the old earth was done years before, in 2014. It was important to the masters that anyone going to the new world would leave with exceptional energy. Their energy had to be of a high vibration because only that kind of energy would survive the new world, StarDrome.

She was a distant planet starving for love and affection. The masters didn't know if she was accepting of new inhabitants. The masters worked and studied with her energetically for years before she settled down from her negative energies because of galactic wars.

StarDrome provoked changes to each cell soul's skin so it became tougher and more elastic; Creating skin texture to match StarDrome's energy; so it was compatible to the planet's changes in recent years.

The planet was chosen for healing and for the purpose of the gifted ones to come and teach the old ways. The masters had seen all of these things transpire in their visions, when they were all small and learning as well. The masters were all taught by their parents and teachers too, about this new day coming and the things they needed to prepare.

The masters' house all the gifts the mentors carry and sometimes a different master would have two or three gifts, if not four. Their abilities were endless, but they were aging and knew that the mentors that followed them will soon hold their space.

It depended on the teachings and what each master was born to do. There would be a council meeting coming soon with all the masters and their mentors. This meeting would take place in the Core of StarDrome; the core was the only meeting place for the masters and the mentors.

The Core was sanctified as they believed things were kept holy and the energy was decent there. The core was a lavish beautiful burgundy and golden room, the place was massive and guardians stood in the doorways, which were in four directions.

Each guardian was bathed in white and silver light. The light was so bright, that each master and mentor had to switch their sight to lower frequency energy, just by saying "vision down" when they entered.

Then their eyes would automatically adjust to suit each person's energy and what the body's system needed. This was the holiest space that any cell sensed or captured through their essence…

13

The Core

The Healing Place of Splendor

The Core had a huge circular table in the center of the room. The room was buzzing with anticipation and love. The energy of adoration was felt within the warmth of the sun through the Core, it is so beautiful.

The energy of gold and plum radiated through each heart and opened up all those wonderful gifts, through each mentor. The energy spun around the room and set balance with all the mentors, masters and with each person who came into the Core.

Anyone who came to the Core would receive a healing through this tremendous ray of light, from the top of the head down their entire body. Sometimes, Sly would curl his toes and try to hold a straight face, but to his dismay, Luna would laugh at him.

She couldn't help herself because Sly was cute in her eyes and once Luna did that, he couldn't stop smiling and laughing with her. But, they had to remind each other telepathically to pay attention and be serious within this sacred space.

Next thing you know, all the mentors were chuckling and Sly was red in the face, embarrassed. But Sly knew if that made Luna happy, well, that's all that mattered. Then Sly knew in his heart that Luna loved him, even if she didn't say it to him yet.

But Sly sends Luna a beautiful energy of soft butterflies, and she just melted and was very pleased and relaxed into the energy…

Angel made sure she sat right beside Justice before any mentor noticed. But Angel already knew, she and Justice were reprimanded already, so they needed to be careful, especially if they were sitting in the Core.

Mazie had to be careful by not putting anyone to sleep with her pollen. She was harnessing her abilities and getting better; it was just when she saw Adam, she couldn't help herself.

Mazie had a deep connection with Adam because he would visit her at night, once a week, sometimes twice a week, for a short time. It was forbidden for Adam to be with Amanda because they were brother and sister through marriage.

Adam's father married Amanda's mother in the old world. As Amanda's mother Cheryl was a widow early in her life, at age 19. She bore only one child before Amanda, and lost it in childbirth. Amanda was spoiled in the old world and she had to learn to adapt and let go of old habits. She was forewarned many times to straighten out or she would be transferred to the Island.

That is why Mazie was happy to have her visits with Adam any chance she got, so they could both be with each other and work through their lessons and practices together, and share their daily routines.

It seemed to be that Mazie didn't quite get Amanda's approval to date or see Adam. She knew the consequences if Amanda found out about her and Adam's connection, as there was one long kiss in October, one night. When both of them came together through this kiss, it snowed lightly. The snow touched the ground and created a wonderful white blanket.

The blanket looked like stardust. But it only snowed that once, that is why it is so special for both Mazie and Adam. No one could get tired from Mazie's pollen in the winter. The energy between Mazie and Adam was pure because no one made it snow on StarDrome before…

The masters claimed the snow came and wouldn't be seen again, unless the planet shifted out of alignment, just like when the old earth was going through devastation. Adam introduced his true self to Mazie under a full moon, as he always left her with good intentions so she good return at his favorite time of night.

They decided to keep their kiss secret because they both knew their energies made it snow. Then the masters wouldn't question it again unless they made it snow again…Adam's powers were increasing as he saw Mazie. His powers to shape-shift were at their peak, especially when there was a moon.

Adam shifted into a black alpha wolf; his long, strong, muscular legs were so quietly there, as he crept over to Mazie and howled. Mazie never noticed Adam until he leaped at her to play; Mazie screamed with fright and said telepathically to Adam, "Oh my God, just let me know when you're going to do that to me, as I wasn't prepared."

How do you know where I am if I change my colors to match the terrain? She candidly said to Adam, and then she sprayed yellow pollen at him. It landed on top of his forehead, she chuckled because it looked like Adam had yellow in his black hair – well, his black fur.

Mazie mentioned to Adam, "That is a swell look for you, Adam! You look good in yellow!"

Then Adam spoke with a deep voice to Mazie, "Call me Dexter the Black." And he jumped up and over to Mazie over to her right side and said, "get up on my back and I'll take you for a ride."

Mazie agreed temporarily, as long as she wasn't out for a long period of time, because the doors close on the Blocks at 10pm, and once the doors close, everything is in lockdown on StarDrome.

Mazie jumped on to Dexter's back and then rode off into the night. Adam and Mazie smiled so deeply, reassured that they would be back on time. Then all of a sudden, Mazie heard Master Winged One shout, "Excuse me Mazie we're all here, just speaking about this trance you both go into, we're all in the Core."

Then Mazie spiritually jumped back into her body and realized she was gone for some time. She realized that she could have astral projected into her memories of Adam. This surprised Mazie as it did Master Shade and the others.

The masters once again remind all the mentors to keep present and to breathe.

This will keep them in their bodies and retain their energy systems while there in the Core, and then they all remain aware of what's taking place in the Core with others...

The masters nodded and pointed to the big books in front of each mentor. Then Master Hedge Hog said telepathically in a stern voice, "this is your training manual and you all have been writing in this journal while you were working through your lessons.

Make sure everything is written in it, regarding the things you teach your students. Make sure that it is full and in detail and that your students signed off on their lessons or the lessons need to be repeated."

The mentors nodded as Master Hedge Hog shared and they immediately looked deeply through their journals. Then Master could sense how much energy went into the teachings, the mentors taught their students daily.

Master was happy to see how much the students were learning, at an advanced level. A couple of lessons needed to be repeated by Adam and Sage, well for Andrew, too, but otherwise, all is well in the Core.

The meeting was a success as Master Hedge Hog shared with the other Masters in circle. There was another reminder for Mazie, so she could remember to stay grounded during any meetings in the future. Master Silver Cloud quietly shared with Mazie and Adam, so everything was kept sacred.

Mazie and Adam were glad that master Shade respected their lessons, as he did with all other mentors. Then they sent energy of appreciation to all the masters in the Core, and then thanked all the other mentors as well.

Each meeting in the Core was to keep things updated, so there were no surprises to anyone on StarDrome. Each mentor with each master, from each different Block was present at the meeting. It was imperative for all attendees to make sure all lessons were taught and recorded in the journals.

Plus, the keys for each journal were checked by Master Knightley in private; because each key was unique for each mentor…everything was excellent for the Masters, so they could pass the information to the Old Teacher – Monkey Dances.

Then he would mark passed and continue to write all this knowledge in the book of Life. It was a good day in the Core for everyone who attended; there is still a lot of new work to be done on StarDrome.

Then the closing ceremonies' took place to honor each soul present, the mentors all felt good as they left, and the masters felt good too, because everything was on track, just the way they chose…

14

Celebrations – Coming Together

Marriage, Teachers, Mentors

Three years have passed in StarDrome, and it was the year of the great fasting before the great feast. As all the mentors were graduating from all their roles, some were moving on to get married.

Their marriages took place by order of the ascended masters because each cell had a vibrational energy that was matched to each couple; so they could share a star-seed together.

It was imperative since birth that each person chosen was to come together at the great feast, not before, or this would create a slower moving energy, for each couple. The masters had to have everything in alignment because the lessons involved carried tremendous healing.

Each mentor was taught intensively by each master, so the emotional burdens and energies still leftover from the old earth, wouldn't interfere with the lessons they taught their students.

Each soul passed rigorous teachings to come this far so the mentors were designated to new roles and new mentors came forth, from other Blocks. Now these new mentors will teach what they know and move forward like their mentors did before them.

Some mentors will also move on for strict teachings to become a master, as the masters were aging fast and whatever the masters taught remained with the mentors coming into mastership.

The teachings could only carry forward through them now, so the masters before them needed to be certain on who they chose to continue. Only those mentors who hold their high esteem in gratitude can continue to teach.

StarDrome is being prepared for the festivities in a couple of days, for all the ones fasting are in the northeast side of StarDrome.

They will come out refreshed and ready for their new responsibilities. The women and men from Block F and B are setting up the round tables for everyone. There is a lot of fruit from the trees that is being offered on the far right. It is being spread out on the longest table in the front of StarDrome's cabbage trees.

You could see big copper plates infused with a twinge of blue and red color, being used as the offering plates. This was StarDrome's way of honoring all the souls who passed on to new worlds and civilizations. Then each cell would give a gift and set it on the plate with their intentions for love and peace.

The food that was offered was of great significance for all the mentors and teachers and masters, to honor all things taught to them since arriving in the new world. The tables were draped in pale pink cotton with pretty flowers.

Some tables were draped with a peach color and purple flowers, with white cotton underneath. In the center of each table was a fresh bouquet of flowers picked by Sage and all the younger rainbow children.

Each crystal child decided to place a crystal on each table to mark the occasion. The smells and aroma filled the air, as the energy of delight was felt by everyone including Augustine and Kira in the Bad Lands.

They could sense something big happening in StarDrome. They both could feel the energy of excitement, joy, peace and love. They both grinned with glee because they both missed StarDrome's festivities, because they had to create their own in the Bad Lands.

Augustine and Kira wanted to go home, to leave the Bad Lands behind as they both filled their time there. They both proceeded to transmit messages to that side of StarDrome, to see who would hear them or see them in their visions. There was no reply because the masters created an energy beam that shot down over StarDrome, to protect it from any outside interference.

Adam and Amanda were singing, and fixing the podium where the masters would be seated. On each side of the podium the mentors will sit around the masters to honor them. Adam felt something awkward just then, it was a faint voice or buzzing sound in his ear, the energy felt familiar to him.

But he shrugged it off because it didn't feel just right at that moment. Within that moment the two mentors felt someone tune in but the transmission was lost…

Andrew created warm winds for the feast so he knew everything had to be just right.

He could see that Justice and Angel were frolicking in the back of the healing room while everyone was busy.

Tanis and Judy were busy helping in the gourmet kitchen, dishing out the food. Everyone's favorite dish was made.

Luna was helping Sly with his preparations, his speech to the masters, and Luna had her speech for Sly.

Sly had a very personal note to gift Luna, as it was their happiest day on StarDrome. Not just for graduation but for their union and coming together through ancient ceremonies. Sly and Luna knew that they were destined to be together since birth, even though Luna tried very hard to conceal it from Sly.

Everyone knew on StarDrome who was meant to be together, they could sense she liked him and was fond of her SpiderBoy. Luna had a big surprise to share with Sly on their special night, as well. But, she vowed to keep it 'secret' until they were wed.

She was going to open her beautiful white wings and wrap them around her new husband and fly off with him. Luna's gift to Sly was her pure energy as a white Pegasus. She had this discussion with her mother in spirit, as the Pegasus is the most amazing gift ever.

Plus, Luna has been planning quietly with Jamie, her intention to go to the Badlands, to help her friends. Even knowing that it was risky, she still wants to go with Sly. She just hasn't told him yet and the masters already think it's a bad idea.

The masters said to anyone with interest to go to the Bad Lands, that there was a lot of preparation involved. It wasn't one of those things you do in the spur of the moment, because the energies have changed a lot since their arrival on StarDrome.

Then the masters shared with the cell souls, that if anyone needed to go, it would be the masters first, because this way they can prepare the other mentors for their return. But, apparently there was a spiritual process for each of them, coming and going to the Bad Lands.

Luna felt she had good cause, as they have spent a lot of time there already, and she misses them. Plus, Gordon shared a little information about the Bad Lands and how much work was already completed, by all of them.

This way he could ease the responsibilities for the masters, but it was going to take much more than that, Gordon realized. Luna felt a little out of sorts about this request but she knew that the quest was good for her and her soon to be new husband.

Luna was also excited about SpiderBoy's ride on her back, since he knew how to hang on now. Then she smiled to herself and thought,' what an amazing gift'. Luna smiles quietly as she remembers when Sly fell off her back, when they were younger.

But it was his webs that kept him safe.

Luna knew that everyone needed to rest before the final day came and all the things were prepared. Everyone felt exhausted as it was early rise tomorrow, to begin the sacred ceremonies.

Everyone went to rest for the evening, excited about the next day's festivities. All the cells from all the Blocks on StarDrome, created a wonderful place to celebrate. The energy of healing rainbow colors, were felt as everyone drifted to sleep.

The birds were singing and the fairies were dancing, as StarDrome prepared through the night for what was to come. The water beings were jumping through the water with glee and excitement for SpiderBoy.

They were proud of him and all the work he did with his students and StarDrome was humming too! The trees were stepping and moving through the streams and the leaves were rustling within the warm winds, which Wind Walks created.

Everything was ready…for tomorrow's ceremonies.

15

Luna and SpiderBoy

- Taken -

The day came for the great feast. Everyone from Block E and G were up early, as everyone had assigned tasks. The newlyweds weren't permitted to see each other until later so Luna, Angel, Judy, and Mazie went to the South Room to wait and get ready for the festivities.

All of the grandmothers and mothers were there in apparition to help the women get ready for the ceremonies.

Angel stepped out of the South Room quietly, to go see Justice, giggling to herself as she left for a brief moment. The women were so preoccupied, they didn't notice Angel leave.

Luna was with Mazie watching the squirrels assist Cora, as she had many errands that morning and didn't like to be disturbed. Cora loved getting things ready for any festivity as she scurried past Luna and Mazie, as they shared common interests.

Cora reminded them both to get ready, as there was a lot to do. Both girls nodded and knew Cora was right, they were both sharing their happy times together and needed to appreciate all things in that moment.

Mazie could hear Judy looking for her, so she could finish doing her hair. Then Mazie said, 'I'm coming Judy' then she had to leave to go help Judy with her hair because Mazie had the flowers Judy liked.

Luna was left alone admiring the warm sun and she could hear all the things happening within the festivities.

Then all of a sudden Luna saw a bowl of raspberries down by the brook. She felt in that moment maybe somebody had left it there by mistake because there was so much going on for the feast.

Luna felt hungry after the fast and she just wanted one raspberry to pass the time. She thought to herself that it wouldn't hurt, so she bent down to pick the bowl up as her stomach growled. Then all of a sudden, she heard a gust of wind above her head and there was a flash of red…

Luna closed her eyes instantly to protect herself, then she dropped the bowl of raspberries immediately and before she was aware of what was happening, she was picked up by Roth.

She didn't even have time to put her wings out even though she was saving that for Sly. She didn't even have the opportunity to shape-shift, as her thoughts were on her wedding and what Sly might do.

Luna then decided to quiet her thoughts so Sly couldn't sense her or pick up on her thoughts. A few minutes later Mazie came back to get Luna as they were all ready to go to the ceremonies.

Mazie and Judy saw the broken bowl and the raspberries all over the ground. They both looked at each other and thought it was unusual, because no one was due to eat until after the ceremonies, so why were the raspberries all over? Angel let out a dreadful cry and then proceeded to fly back with Justice and leave the ceremonies.

Everyone was shocked to hear Angels cry, as she needed to be careful with her energy, her screams were heard across StarDrome. She spoke out loud in her own voice and screamed, while her body was shaking.

"Roth picked up Luna! He's taking her back to the Bad Lands. Hurry we've got to get her back, we've got to get her some help!"

Then Justice yelled back, "I will go and help her."

Then he ran and shape-shifted into Dray, which was short for Dragon. Then Angel started to cry and she said, "Don't go, Dray! Don't go! That's what Roth wants.

He wants you to go there. Please stay, please stay, and then we can talk to the masters." The energy could be felt all over StarDrome, that Luna was taken. The festivities came to a halt immediately.

Sly came running over to the group of mentors, yelling, "They have Luna! They have Luna! My beloved!

Then all of a sudden Sly was saddened, then the masters said, "wait, wait.

We must discuss this together as a planet." Then the mentors asked, "Who has Luna?" Then Sly said, "Roth has my beloved wife. Roth has a vendetta against the masters, and Justice.

Roth took Luna in to the Bad Lands, knowing it was the perfect time, with no warning." Roth was aware of the celebrations and knew it would be the best time to catch everyone off guard.

Somehow he broke through the barriers the Masters created, Roth has all these plans and desires for Luna, as he draws closer to the Badlands. The other mentors didn't realize what Roth was up too, but they would surely find out.

The energy was changing through the Bad Lands, as Kira could see the vegetation turning to a different color. She ran to tell the others and before she got to the clearing by the rock face she saw Andrew and he was trying to calm the winds.

He could sense the winds were upset and he motioned to talk to them and got throw a few feet from where Kira first saw him. She ran over to help him get up and then they both looked at the face of the grandfather winds and heard them say,' something has happened and this will create a disturbance between the Bad Lands and all the work that went into healing StarDrome.

'Go and prepare the others, as Roth is coming with an uninvited guest.' Then the grandfather winds left in a puff of darken energy and both Kira and Andrew could see the sun, again. Then Kira said to Andrew, 'what has Roth done to create such upset on StarDrome?'

Andrew replied,' it must be something Master Stoney could explain, let's go back to camp and see.' Then they proceeded with caution and they both felt intuitively that the energy has definitely shifted, because they couldn't feel the energy of Peace.

Kira had a tear in her eye and thought quietly,' We all created a wonderful place here since we came and it's all going to be destroyed.' As Kira was thinking those thoughts, Andrew noticed the waterfalls changing color and they started to emit a strange smell.

They arrived to camp to see it upside down and Master Stoney was doing some energy repair and said telepathically to everyone,' go to the healing cave, now!'

'Until we can figure out what has happened here, then he sends for his two helpers.

Luckily Master Stoney was passing through on his way to the ceremonies and his two helpers Jonas and Wendy were acting peculiar, as they were on route. They were flying in all directions and lost sense of where they were going.

Master then guided them to the Bad Lands because he knew where the portal was in case of emergencies. The masters were aware of many things but chose to keep things quiet. Now, it seemed the Bad Lands was in jeopardy as far as master could tell, the energy was definitely strange and indifferent...

Meanwhile Luna could hear Roth's thoughts and he was surely thinking of dreadful things as Luna listened. She felt that Roth was confused, angry and could become hostile and she heard him think,' I haven't been with a woman in so long... and his thoughts were all over the place, as Luna could see his pictures playing out in front of her like a movie.

These were frightening clips and she cried profusely...she had to remind herself to keep silent power, as SpiderBoy could hear and feel everything, she was experiencing...she didn't want him going crazy.

Roth was nervously thinking of impregnating Luna so she could have his seed, not SpiderBoy. This way he could rule through his child and Luna started to cry and felt helpless, and kept sending thoughts of her dying love to Sly.

No matter what; things will be taken care of soon... Sly felt everything Luna was feeling and he dropped to his knees. With his head in his hands he profusely howled,' why take Luna now Roth? 'Why?'

Sly could feel her fear and he had never felt that energy ever. Sly thought to himself and said out loud "What is all of this training for? What?" In Sly's mind, his thoughts are running wild.

He does his best to comfort them through his spiritual tools but can't quiet them. He yells for Master Shades help and realizes he must save Luna, and the masters said to the mentors, "we must all get together. I want a lockdown in all the Blocks.

'Make sure that everyone is going back to their Blocks please, and then the masters and the mentors will come together in the core, and we'll discuss what it is that we need to do." 'Go now and assist as many as you can'.

Master Shade could sense the emotions cursing through SpiderBoy and helped him get up.

SpiderBoy screamed and tried to break free from Master Shade, 'let me go help her, she is my wife to be'. Master Shade was calling out to the other masters to assist in finding out how Roth could have done such a disrespectful thing.

He could feel the sadness through StarDrome and knew they had to work quickly, so she wasn't going to react through war, to protect them all. StarDrome was a planet and she changed many things in energy to protect what she loved.

Master could sense she was upset and he wanted to go help her settle down but had to tend to Sly and what just happened with Luna. SpiderBoy wanted to save his wife, and that's all had in his mind, as Master Shade tuned in to Sly's thoughts.

The masters tried to console SpiderBoy and let him know that he couldn't' go into the Badlands with all that anger, or any of those old emotions. Because it would create an energy that no one liked and what they never thought StarDrome would feel ever again,' war...

Sly couldn't shake off the things he was feeling as he felt Luna strongly telepathically, he could hear her every thought. He was determined to stop Roth, no matter what the masters said or required of him.

The thoughts drove him crazy but it was his visions that were most disturbing... he didn't want those things happening to Luna, so he knew he needed to save her.

Sly telepathically called to all his friends willing to help him get Luna back...and they all heard loud and clear while excusing the Masters warnings... they choose to leave right away and go to the Bad Lands and suffer the consequences later...

Does SpiderBoy save Luna? Or does he risk their fate...

16

The Band Lands

The Battle Begins

SpiderBoy and other cells that chose to go with him prepared for their journey. There was a disturbance of energy on StarDrome now and everyone must choose to keep their authentic power.

Through their very gifts of telepathic and telekinesis energy or risk adapting back to the mind... The very thing that created disease and turmoil on the Old Earth... The mentors were taught since birth about their natural abilities since leaving old earth; they can prepare now for their journey to the Bad Lands.

But, will they choose to use their power in the negative or the positive, the choice is theirs... It is important for the masters to insure that everyone who is choosing to assist SpiderBoy be well trained...

Under any circumstances no one shall leave StarDrome in an emotional distress or it will bring horrendous damage to everything on StarDrome. Similar energy was left on Old Earth because of the lower vibrations of pain and suffering... The practice is to remain calm, peaceful and use their energy wisely for positive...

Does SpiderBoy and others listen to the warning? Or do they proceed into the Bad Lands without the masters by their side?

The story continues…

White Elk Medicine Woman

My Blessings

With blessings as we move forward to create the new cover for – The Bad Lands –

Please feel free to join us, in our quest to introduce 'StarDrome 2024' SpiderBoy into the world...I created phases for each novel in my series... a host of new characters and action packed fun.

Feel free to check me out:

Rosie Trakostanec - Canada | LinkedIn

ca.linkedin.com/in/presenttimealternatives

Rosie Trakostanec (@Spiritconnectio) on Twitter

Present Time - The Sacred Tool to Quiet the Mind by Rosie Trakostanec

http://www.amazon.ca

http://www.amazon.com

Rosie Trakostanec/White Elk Medicine Woman

presenttimealternatives@gmail.com

http://Facebook.comRosieTrakostanec

I thank the creator and all my relatives always! ☺

My gratitude and appreciation to A.D for her speedy work in the transcription of my mp3's.

Thank you to Grandmother White Dove Woman for her kindness and wisdom; special prayers are going out for her beloved pet that recently passed.

Thank you to Grandmother Buffalo Woman/Tricia M for her review and edit and her faith and continued support with my work.

A special thank you to White Butterfly Woman/Joelle P for her review of this novel and for her support in my work, all these years.

Plus, I would also like to thank my dear friends Paula and Taleetha T for their review and continued support in my passion. Also wonderful smiling Charlene and family, thank you!

Thank you Grandmother Yellow Moon/Sandra H for her copy edits and reviews of my novel. Thanks for your bright smile and encouraging words.

ABOUT THE AUTHOR

My name is Rosie White Elk Medicine Woman; I'm a traditional grandmother who walks the Red Road. My journey has been extensive with many wonderful teachings, in the last thirty years. I'm humble to know I came this far on my path, as I have overcome many challenges. I honor the spirit of all those ones I walk with as I'm grateful for where I'm in my journey.

To trust who you become takes practice every day; we meet so many delightful souls along the way and some not so delightful. But it is our practice as spiritual beings to change things for the better, any chance we get. It is choice and it is choice that brought me here to this place in my journey.

Things come to life if you just give it a chance, we don't know until we try and I did; through all of my novels. I look forward to sharing these series with my wonderful readers and their circles.

You can even read the story out loud to your children and let your imagination take you away to a distant world.

I look forward to sharing these wonderful series with my children and grandchildren. I always loved things creative and inspiring and love to share these things with others.

It empowers who we are as souls has we are on an amazing journey of our own. Since the beginning of time we have been on many wonderful journeys and will continue to grow and shine. I'm proud to be here today doing what I love, it's always been my passion to write. I trusted it no matter what I was told because I knew I had something to share.

This novel takes you on a journey to a new place where it holds many new beginnings. The magic and intrigue of my characters unfold as they learn how to honor their gifts as shape shifters, medicine carriers, indigo etc. To be taught, to teach and grow in harmony to strengthen their surroundings and abide by planetary law is practice for some. I include my teachings into the novel as a Medicine Woman to honor the creator for all that is here to receive and share.

Rosie Trakostanec/White Elk Medicine Woman

Public Speaker/Shaman/Master Practitioner of the Healing Arts

Available for speaking engagements –

presenttimealternatives@gmail.com

CPSIA information can be obtained
at www.ICGtesting.com
Printed in the USA
LVHW081501291220
675335LV00034B/1005